John C Cole was born in Waukesha, Wisconsin, in 1971. He was raised in Boston, Massachusetts, and he studied creative writing and literature at the University of Massachusetts, Boston. He currently teaches composition and writing courses at Colorado Mesa University and at Quincy College in Massachusetts. John is also the author of *The Lost Words*, a collection of short stories and prose.

For Bob and Jo
May the wind always be at your back.

John C Cole

BLUEJAY IN THE ATTIC

AUSTIN MACAULEY PUBLISHERS™

LONDON • CAMBRIDGE • NEW YORK • SHARJAH

Ordering Information
Quantity sales: Special discounts are available on quantity purchases by corporations, associations, and others. For details, contact the publisher at the address below.

Publisher's Cataloging-in-Publication data
Cole, John C
Bluejay in the Attic

ISBN 9798889109587 (Paperback)
ISBN 9798889109600 (ePub e-book)
ISBN 9798889109594 (Audiobook)

Library of Congress Control Number: 2023921645

www.austinmacauley.com/us

First Published 2024
Austin Macauley Publishers LLC
40 Wall Street, 33rd Floor, Suite 3302
New York, NY 10005
USA

mail-usa@austinmacauley.com
+1 (646) 5125767

The following story is based on actual events.
Certain names and situations have been changed,
fictionalized,
or dramatized for the sake of anonymity
and creative storytelling.

After Andy's funeral, my mother and I sat at her kitchen table drinking hot tea with lemon and honey. We still had our black clothes on, and there was nothing much to say as we quietly sat there. I was wrapping the string of my tea bag around the spoon when we heard the fluttering and flapping in the attic. "That damn bird," said my mother. "This is the third or fourth time this month. Could you please do me a favor and go and try to get it out?"

I finished my tea and changed my clothes. I pulled the string to the attic stairs and climbed the ladder. I tugged the pull-string light overhead and looked around for the bird. It stayed hidden and quiet for a long time, and I stayed hidden and quiet for a long time too. I spent nearly twelve hours in the attic that day. I eventually found the bird, but I found much more than that while I was up there.

We all deal with death in our own personal way, but sometimes we need help. Sometimes we need someone to show us how. My brother, Andy, was twenty-nine when he died, and this is the story of how he helped me come to terms with his death.

1

"Six months is a long time to go without loving you," she said, "and I'm not sure I can handle that."

Her mild threats had always turned me on, and it wasn't the first time she said something like that to me. I pulled her down onto our bed for maybe the last time. She let me love her like we do, and her eyes revealed the silent war that was playing out in her mind. Will she wait for me, or will she leave me? I could tell she loved me and hated me all at once. She said nothing as I moved about her. I could see the tears forming in her eyes. I knew she questioned my love for her. I told her that I'd be back, but she turned her head toward the wall, telling me to leave.

So long, I thought, to my girlfriend and those long nights of waiting tables and tending bar. My time had come to go. She refused to smile as I packed my things on the bedroom floor. Her tears were like raindrops on car windows—the streaks left marks on her pale, dry face. She all but begged me not to go, and she wouldn't promise to be there when I got back. She knew her mild threats had an effect on me.

My friend, Robert, honked out front as I shouldered my bag and looked at her naked in our bed. She'd been resenting me ever since I decided to go, and she'd been detaching more and more from me each day. We were both waiting for that moment of leaving, and when it arrived, it was like we were oceans apart, with nothing but unsettled water between us. I didn't know what to say to the girl I shared nearly everything with. That moment of silence was like no other—it was dead wind at sea.

I cleared my throat before leaving. "Perhaps I'll see you in six months," I said, closing the door behind me. I walked down the driveway to Robert's car, and I could feel the silent war taking place inside of me. I was sad to leave her, but excited for the months to come.

Robert smiled but didn't say anything as he drove north on I-95 out of Florida. As we crossed the state line to Georgia, he said, "I envy you, ya know. And I'd do just about anything to tag along with you."

"I asked if you wanted to come," I said.

"I know. I know you did, man. I'm just saying."

"I get it," I said. "Maybe next time."

The sun began to set as Robert adjusted the visor above the dash to keep out the sun's rays. We drove quietly following signs to Atlanta. I stared into the darkening horizon as I rethought my reasons for leaving.

I've seen the same things and I've had the same thoughts for a few years now. I've talked over and over again with all the people at the bar, night after night, day after day, and nobody cares anything about adventure anymore. Nobody cares about taking off, exploring, and taking chances. Seems like nobody wants to go anywhere anymore. People have become so vanilla in the town I live in. Computer screen vanilla. Barroom vanilla. And the kids in my neighborhood walk around in boredom and torn blue jeans—earrings in their faces, as they stare into cell phones to check social media likes.

Everything seems to be dying in the town I live in, and the playgrounds there have rotted away with tall grass that needs cutting. The youth sit around on rusted-out swing sets and seesaws with untied shoes and cigarettes burning. They show off new tattoos and pictures of their most recent squeeze. To them, adventure means new ink on their forearms and maybe getting laid. Heroin is everywhere. Fentanyl is everywhere. The fog is thick, and the evening news speaks of so many kids never reaching adulthood.

When I look at the lazy, addicted days of this younger generation, I realize that I'm getting too old for rusted-out playgrounds and getting high. I'm too old for keg parties in the woods and getting my girl's name branded on my Facebook forearm.

And that's why I left her. I left when I did because I'm getting too old for all that shit. And, who knows, God just might see fit to put me in some corporate suit and tie sometime soon. I left when I did because I wanted to live a little bit before the nine-to-five office grind bogged me down. I left because I wanted to explore some of this world before she came to me with the proposition of a family and a mortgage. I wanted to stretch my legs and run around a little bit before that diamond ring shortened my bank account. I wanted to take some chances and breathe some fresh mountain air before the gray started showing up in my beard. The truth is, I left when I did because I never wanted to sound like Robert. I never want to say, "I wish I'd gone with you, man."

Atlanta sparkled up ahead as the southbound traffic began to thin along the highway. I pulled two cigarettes from my pocket as Robert cracked the window and handed me his lighter. "You gonna quit smoking out there?" he asked.

We both sat back in our seats and inhaled the smoke. "I dunno," I said. "Sure would make things easier if I did."

"You wanna stop off in the city for a drink?" he said, nudging my shoulder, laughing.

"Yeah, right," I said. "We'll never get there if we do that."

The lights of Atlanta sparkled as we passed them by. I felt captured by all my thoughts as the butterflies began to swim around in my belly. I smoked. Atlanta looked clean that night, and the passing cars used blinkers before they cut us off. Robert drove his rusted-out Honda at fifty-five miles per hour in the passing lane, but he didn't care, and I didn't care, because we both knew it would be a long time before I saw the lights of any city flicker like that again.

I met Robert a year earlier in a Jacksonville Beach coffee shop. I stood behind him in line one morning as he asked for a "cauffee with sugah." The pudgy donut lady behind the counter leaned forward with that *say again* look in her eye, and Robert leaned in and slowly repeated, "cauufffeee with sugggaahhh." The donut lady shook her head while pouring his cup, and I introduced myself as being from the same neck of the northeast woods.

Robert had grown up some fifty miles south of me in Providence, and he'd only been in Florida for three months before meeting me. Initially, he told me he was in Florida for work, but a month or so later, he told me the real reason why he was there. He owed too much money to too many different bad guys, and he was in too deep with the drugs and the alcohol. The ladies, the family bullshit, and the little girl of his that he never saw… I just smiled and laughed to myself because I, too, had similar reasons for being in Florida. We'd both grown up as bad kids in bad parts of town, and being tough guys was starting to catch up to us. We both knew that prison cells didn't have doors that swung both ways, and we both wanted more out of life than the other kids in our neighborhoods. We both realized that hanging around on the streets of Boston and Providence would lead to nothing more than pregnant girlfriends and prison numbers. We liked each other immediately, Robert and me, because we both shared the common experience of getting out while there was still time. We both felt lucky that way.

Robert was at least half black, with dark skin and short, curly hair. He wore a thin beard that was tight to his face, and hoop earrings in both ears. He was thirty or so pounds overweight. Truth be told, Robert didn't even know what his background was, or who his original parents were. Foster home gave him a number when he was still in diapers, and one day a Mexican couple looked through a window and said they wanted number forty-two or some shit like that. Hell of a way to come into the world, if you ask me, and Robert didn't like talking about it much.

"So, it must be tough leaving Jada like this," he said, flicking his cigarette out the window.

"More than you know, my brother. More than you know."

"Do you love her?" he asked.

"Ah man, I don't know," I said. "I've been asking myself the same thing for a while now, and sometimes I wonder who I'm running from, her or me?"

"Maybe you're not running at all, man? Maybe you're just doing something you wanna do?"

"Yeah, maybe," I said.

"Ah, come on now, man! Don't give me that 'yeah, maybe' bullshit. I mean, who was the guy that I listened to about being honest with myself and finding some hope in this fucked-up world we're living in? It was you, man. It was you that I followed around like some lost fucking puppy dog while I was trying to get clean, so don't give me that 'yeah maybe' bullshit! Do you love her or not?"

I looked over at Robert as he drove but didn't say anything.

Sometime later he said, "And now I'm watching you take this fuckin' trip, and man, you're goddamn right, I'm jealous. And I wish I could go with you, but I can't. I just can't. But that doesn't mean I don't admire what you're doing. Hell, I admire the shit out of what you're doing, because I'll tell you right now, I don't have the sack to do what you're doing. If I had a girl like Jada at home waiting on me, and a place like yours to live in, there ain't no way I'd leave. Sorry dog, but there ain't no way I'm leaving that."

"Tell it like it is," I said, trying to make light of things.

"Fuck you," he said.

"No, you're right," I said. "You're right. It's just kinda funny hearing all this from you. I mean, a few months ago, you were sitting there all full of self-pity and bullshit, and now you're trying to live right and give a little something back. I'm gonna miss you, bro. I really am. But I feel like this is something I gotta do. And if she loves me, then she'll be there when I get back. And if I love her, then maybe I'll come back."

We both laughed. "You're coming back," he said, slapping my shoulder.

"Yeah," I said. "I'll be back."

"That is, if you don't get swallowed up by some big fuckin' grizzly or some shit."

"You ain't kidding," I said.

Signs for Gainesville, Georgia were up ahead, and I held my mini flashlight over my trail map because Robert's interior light didn't work. We lost cell service once we got into the mountains, so his phone couldn't tell us where to go. "Highway Fifty-Two should be up here on the right," I said, looking over my map, and Robert slowed the car down to like twenty miles an hour and started looking for the turn. A big truck grew impatient behind us and started flashing high beams, and Robert shouted for the guy to go fuck himself as he passed us by.

"Fucking trucks," he said. "People just need to relax."

"You were going like fifteen miles an hour," I said, laughing.

"Fuck you too," said Robert. "Hey, how come you didn't have me drop you off in the morning or afternoon? I'd love to see these mountains in the daylight. I bet it's some kind of beautiful up here."

"I dunno, man. It is what it is. Come on, let's go," I said. "The road we want is up ahead."

"But the air, man! Can you smell that? It smells so clean up here."

"Yeah," I said. "It really goes great with my smoking! Come on, let's go."

"It's fucking cold, though," he said. "It must be like twenty degrees or something. You sure you got enough clothes with you? I'd hate to see you freeze out there and then have some park ranger call me up saying my buddy is frozen solid to a mountain in Tennessee or some shit."

"I have clothes," I said.

"You sure you don't want my coat, man? Come on, take my coat. And every time you put it on, you can think of me working fifty-plus hours a week at the office. Come on, you want it?"

"What are you, my friggin' mother?" I said. "No, I don't want your coat. My pack is heavy enough as it is. I'll just keep moving if I'm cold."

"Alright, alright," he said. "I just hope I don't get that call from Mr. Park Ranger. And what about my phone, man? You sure you don't want to take a phone with you?"

"No," I said. "No phones. No technology on this trip. All that fucking technology is destroying our society… Whoa, whoa, wait a sec," I said. "This is it! Turn here! Turn here! This is it."

Amicalola Falls State Park was five miles up some dirt road on the right-hand side. The nighttime silhouette of massive mountains made the road much darker and harder to see, and no streetlights didn't help much either. I felt intimidated by the depth of all the darkness. I could feel my heart racing. I said nothing as Robert's Honda bounced along the dirt and gravel road.

We pulled into the park and Robert turned off the car in front of a log cabin headquarters type place. The front porch light was on, and several large bugs circled the exposed bulb. We got out of the car and stretched our legs. The air was cold, crisp, and clean. The small butterflies in my belly were now large birds chirping in my chest.

The months of planning and waiting were finally over. I was finally there. I knew that Robert would soon be getting back into his Honda and driving away. The wonder of it all was suddenly staring me in the face. The bleacher stairs I climbed every day for training at the Fletcher High School football field were now actual mountains looking down on me. There was no more anticipation or dreamy nights of not being able to fall asleep. I had arrived, and I was standing on the doorstep of the biggest adventure of my life. I was overwhelmed. I pulled two cigarettes from my pack and handed one to Robert. We sat on the front porch steps of the cabin, like old men sometimes do, and we smoked in silence. We listened to the sounds of some nearby waterfall.

"You think you'll be able to stay clean up there in those woods?" he finally said.

"I'll get plenty dirty," I said, "but I think I'll be able to stay clean." We both smirked. "What about you?" I asked. "You think you'll be able to stay clean?"

"I sure hope so, man. I'll have a year in April, so you'd better find a phone somewhere out there to give me a call."

"No shit," I said. "A year in April! Where'd the time go?"

"Sure does fly by when you're not in a blackout!"

"You ain't kiddin'," I said.

Robert helped me pitch my tent beside the log cabin, and then he hopped back into that piece of shit Honda and cranked the engine. "That thing gonna make it back?" I said, shaking my head.

"Fuck you," he said, lighting another cigarette. After a moment of some kind of silence, he said, "Take care, Birdman. Godspeed."

"You got it," I said. "Safe home." Robert cracked a smile and pulled away.

3:33pm

My parents named me John after my grandfather, but my mother and my friends always called me Jay. My grandmother called me Jay-son whenever she was around, and my father called me Weasel because I always stuck my nose where it didn't belong. My sister called me whatever four-letter word was in her vocabulary at the time, but my brother called me Jaybird, always Jaybird.

2

The calendar said it was March 4th. The thermostat on the side of the log cabin said it was 24 degrees. The morning fog hung trapped in the valley like smoke in a small room, and the misty morning air made my tent damp and heavy. The beads of water that ran down the face of my tent reminded me of the tears on Jada's cheeks the day before, and I wondered if I'd ever make her breakfast in bed again. The nearby waterfall sounded louder than it did the night before, and my wool socks scratched the hell out of my feet. My hiking boots felt large, heavy, and clumsy, and goosebumps came to my legs as I hurried to pack my things. A park ranger stepped out of the front door of the cabin and breathed deeply as he pulled up his trousers. He raised his arms above his head with that morning type stretch and he looked my way with a smile on his face. "Sleep well?" he asked.

"Not too bad," I said.

"Are you out to do the whole trail or just a section?" he asked.

"The whole thing, I hope."

"Well, alright then! It's always good to see another thru-hiker," he said. "I hope you have a great hike, and just be sure to sign the logbook before you leave."

"Yep, you bet," I said.

"We've got fresh coffee inside too. If you want some, help yourself."

"Thanks," I said. "I just might do that."

"What's your trail name?" he asked.

"Bird," I said.

He chuckled to himself. "It's funny to think that a bird has a whole lot of walking to do."

"Yeah, I hadn't thought of it like that, but I guess you're right."

"Well, I think it's a great trail name. Have yourself a good hike, Bird."

"Yep. Thanks again."

The fire in the corner of that cabin roared and snapped, and it smelled like the old campfires I remembered from when I was a kid. The Maxwell House coffee wasn't all that fresh, but it felt warm in my hands, and I put extra milk and sugar in it because I knew it would be some time before I tasted those things again. *Sugaaahhhh*, I thought, as I remembered meeting Robert.

A large leather journal sat open on a wooden desk in the corner of the cabin, and I read over a few of the most recent entries. A hiker named Afterburner signed in two days before, on March 2nd, and he let it be known that he wasn't stopping until he hiked the full 2,192 miles to Katahdin, Maine. "Finally here," he wrote. "But man, it's cold! I hope it warms up soon. See you out there. Georgia-to-Maine."

There were about thirty entries made the week or so leading up to mine, and all but one crazy bastard were hiking north. The southbound hiker went by the name of The Wizard, and three days earlier, on March 1st, he pulled into Amicalola Falls after hiking nearly 2,200 miles in the middle of winter. His entry said, "Man, it was cold! I nearly died a couple times out there. I'm glad to be done, and I'm glad I did it, but I'm never doing it again! Maine-to-Georgia. Wizard signing out."

I remember wishing I hadn't read The Wizard's entry, and I remember looking out the back window of that log cabin as a dirt trail curled up and around a few pine trees. I had this feeling that the toughest of all my steps would be the first, so I strapped myself into my pack, took a deep breath, and stepped out the backdoor.

Immediately, I was out of breath. The dirt trail wasted no time twisting its way up and up. My forty-pound pack felt like twice that weight. My lungs started screaming, and I gagged up a mothball-sized clump of phlegm that tasted like coffee. My chest started burning, like it was on fire. And I honestly started questioning myself, for real, wondering if I had made a terrible mistake by coming out to the woods.

It wasn't long though before I was standing on top of the waterfall I had heard the night before. I stood there thinking for a long time—thinking about what my options were. I knew Robert was already back in Florida, and I didn't have a phone, so I couldn't call him. I couldn't call Jada either. And even if I could call them, what would I say? My options were limited, very limited, and I knew it. I refocused. I said some half-assed prayer under my breath because I honestly didn't know what else to do. Then the fear crept in, and I thought about walking back to the log cabin and making another entry about changing my mind. *What the fuck!* I decided to keep walking forward to see what would come of it. Even small children don't quit after only hiking one mile, right?

Four hours of hiking seemed more like twenty-five, and I could taste the salt on my upper lip as the sweat continuously rolled down my face. Then the summit of Springer Mountain appeared out of nowhere, and all the aches and pains, fears and phlegm balls, simply went away. I couldn't feel the burning tightness in my chest and legs anymore because the view from that mountain top created a numbness throughout my body that simply overwhelmed me. The view was like nothing I'd ever seen before. Amazing.

On top of that mountain, I saw a boulder with a metal plaque embedded in its face. It said something about this being the Appalachian Trail, "a place where man creates fellowship with the wilderness." And I pondered over that statement for a while, as I tugged on my water bottle and scoffed down a Snicker's bar. The world looked different from 3,750 feet, and I stood there watching a huge blackbird in flight overhead. It circled high above my place on the summit before adjusting its wings and shooting straight down toward the forest floor below. In amazement, I watched as that bird disappeared into the treetops, and then, seconds later, it returned to the sky with empty claws.

And I thought about those empty claws for a while before realizing I had all the time in the day to think about things like that. There was nothing, absolutely nothing, to disrupt my thinking, and that thought scared the shit out of me.

I pulled a Marlboro from my pack, as I surveyed the trail both north and south. I inhaled and exhaled my smoke. I thought about how much of an idiot I'd feel like if another hiker came along to see me sucking down a cigarette. But that thought eventually fell away as I got caught up in watching the view from the summit. The sky went from baby blue up above to darker shades of purple along the horizon, and the trees below me to the east were turning darker with the late afternoon shade. My body got chillier the longer I stood there, and the sounds of absolute silence rang loud in my ears. But sometimes the wind would kick up and cause the tree limbs to clap and chatter, as if they were trying to say something to me.

The earth around me appeared ready to wake itself from a long winter's nap, and all the trees were trying to push through their tiny green buds. With all those naked trees surrounding me, I could see how hard and jagged the earth actually was. Gray stones of all shapes and sizes were everywhere, and the rust-colored roots of the trees seemed to hug and hold onto them. Everything looked weathered and gray.

I began to feel dirty and exposed on the inside, and I continued to smoke as I thought about why I felt that way. I could identify with the harsh winter rocks and roots surrounding me, and I thought about that a little longer. I thought about the pack of Marlboros I smoked every day and how charred my lungs must have been. I thought about the destructive lifestyle I once lived, and all the effort I put into trying to change that. I thought about how I used to settle for less, and how I'd beat myself up when things didn't go my way. I've always been hard on myself, and in that moment, on that summit, I felt weathered and gray like the woods around me.

I wanted to be happy though, I ready did. I wanted the tiny green buds inside of me to pop up and out, and I wanted life to flower for me. I wanted to feel free, clean, and content, like the old park ranger from that morning... but his peace of mind and big smile were things I didn't have for myself. That park ranger had something I didn't have, and I knew it. I was trying to think my way into feeling better about myself, but everything around me was so gray, sharp, and cold.

I smoked more as my thoughts turned into a couple of hours sitting on that rock. I considered the so-called 'fellowship' that the rock called for. I considered the downward flight of that blackbird and its retreat to the sky with empty claws. I ran my fingers through my hair with a sigh and thought about how trivial it was to compare the empty claws of that bird to my own life.

Then I encountered fear on a much deeper level because I had nothing to distract me from it. There were no TVs or Netflix shows to turn on in the woods. There were no bills to worry about paying in the woods, no girlfriends to comfort me, or cars to maintain. There were no phone calls to answer or social media profiles to update—there was nothing but me, my thoughts, and the ebb and flow of the mountains I would climb.

The sun had moved its way across the sky in the time I sat on that *fellowship* rock, and I needed to move on. My guidebook promised me shelter for the night a few miles north, so I shouldered my pack and carried on.

I heard voices as I approached Stover Creek Shelter, and I could smell the burning wood of a fire. Socks and t-shirts hung from a tree-to-tree clothesline, and the fire roared in the pit as I walked up to the shelter. There were two of them: a young boy, maybe nine or ten years old, and his father. I realized I'd almost gone the entire day without talking to anyone but myself, so I was happy to see them. I was happy for the distraction.

"My name is Little Rock," said the boy, "and this is my father, Rock. What's your name?"

"Hello there, Little Rock. My name is Bird."

The boy chuckled and looked toward his father. "Bird," he said. "That's a cool name. You're hiking up to Maine, Bird?"

"That's the plan, Little Rock. I'm headed up to Maine."

"Wow, that's awesome," he said. "Me and my dad, I mean Rock, are hiking up to Hiawassee, where my mom is gonna pick us up."

"That's great, Little Rock. Maybe someday you'll hike up to Maine too."

"That's right," he said. "Someday I will."

"I'm sure you will."

The boy had freckles and a face that sparkled. It sparkled because his father had taken him into the woods for a week of hiking and discovery. That little boy reminded me of myself some years ago. Rock sat with his legs crossed on the wooden floor of the shelter as he prepared a dinner of macaroni and cheese and chicken from a can. Little Rock sat just like his father, and he had one eye on his dad's every move. He stirred his pot when his dad did. He drank his water when his dad drank. He clicked off his stove and blew on his hot meal the same way his dad did. There was pride on his little face, and he sat there with a straight back and a wide smile as he ate his meal.

I rubbed my tender feet and waited for my own water to boil. Dry clothes on my skin felt like the soft touch of Jada, and the hot meal warmed my insides. There was magic in the eyes of that little boy as he zipped up his sleeping bag and kissed his father goodnight. He more than likely dreamed of growing up to be just like his father, and I, too, had those dreams when I was a kid.

My father used to take me fishing when I was nine or ten, and I remember looking at him through the eyes of Little Rock. I was proud to stand by his side and wear my shirt untucked like he did. I wore my fishing cap like he did, and I wore a belt if he did. I'd spit if he spat. I'd swear if he swore. I started smoking because he smoked, and I drank beer because he let me. My father and I would fish together so we could get away from it all for a while. We'd fish when he called in sick for work, and we fished the New England coastline for blues and bass. We fished streams and ponds for trout and smallmouth bass. I've since learned, however, that my father and I fished for different reasons. He fished to escape life for a little while, and I fished to be just like him. The day would eventually come when we stopped fishing altogether.

I started to understand some of my reasons for being out there in those woods. I understood that I was there to create a bond with nature, yes, but I was also there to create a bond with myself and my past. I would lick my wounds along the way, and I would try my hand at forgiveness as I hiked through unfamiliar places. I looked forward to meeting men like Rock and boys like Little Rock.

The morning was cold and damp, and the low-hanging clouds looked about ready to cry. Little Rock slept snuggled up against Rock, and I packed my things as coffee heated on my stove.

I considered a day of writing beside Stover Creek, but I figured the air was too cold to sit in one spot all day. There would be plenty of time for writing. My fingers tingled in the morning frost, and the coffee felt good in my hands. My breath somehow tasted cleaner than the day before, but it still looked like smoke when I exhaled. I said farewell to the father and son in the shelter logbook, and I left the book open at their feet so they would see. I stood over that little boy for several moments, staring at the youthful smile on his face as he dreamed.

The gray, misty morning turned to steady rain within minutes of my early morning climb, and I asked out loud for the sun to shine. The higher I climbed, the colder it got, and the wind ripped into my face with chunks of frozen rain. I quickly became heavy and saturated. I cursed out loud to whatever God was listening because my simple prayer for some sun was answered with more rain. I knew I should have stayed in my sleeping bag that morning, but I pushed on instead because I wanted to move away from the father and son that reminded me of my father. I needed a new distraction, a new thought.

I started thinking about The Wizard and the reasons why that crazy son of a bitch would choose to hike in winter weather like that. I mean, it felt like Alaska in January to me, and I began to look at the forest around me through the eyes of that Chris McCandless kid, who, back in the 90s, chose to walk out into the Alaskan wilderness by himself. What the hell was that kid thinking? I mean, really? What was he *really* thinking about? Sure, I read that book, and I saw the movie too, but that kid isn't around anymore to answer the simple question of whether he was walking towards himself in nature, or running away from his past? Something on my inside told me that I'd be walking toward my past in a present-tense type way, and I knew it would rain and storm and feel very cold along the way. Something else told me that my past would often make me want to stay in bed for the day. The answer that began to seep its way through to me was that hiking every day was the one thing that would walk me through the weather of my past. But there was so much stormy winter weather on the inside, and I knew it. It made me want to stay in bed.

Once, I decided to sit in the pouring rain behind a shrub in the backyard instead of being in the house where my drunk father was looking for someone to tear into. He had already slapped my sister around some before she took off down the street to her friend's house, and my brother and mother weren't home. It was just me in the house, and I didn't want to give my father the chance to rip someone else apart, so I slipped out the backdoor to hide in the back bushes. And getting soaked that night was fine with me; it was well worth it to me back then.

I never understood my father's violence. There were so many nights where I would listen in bed, and mom and dad just seemed to forget how thin the walls were in our house. Some nights their fights would last until the sun came up, but more often than not, my father would leave the house with screeching tires in the driveway. I'm pretty sure I was old enough to understand that it wasn't me, my brother, or my sister that caused all that anger, but I did spend a good amount of time wondering about that as a kid. And the unpredictability of those nights was a lot like the trail I found myself hiking on in the present moment—only God knew what was up ahead of me. I had no idea what to expect when it came to my father, but I noticed that I was curious, really curious as to what was around the next bend of the trail. So, I hiked on, and I smoked.

I found some shelter under a tight-knit group of pine trees, and the freezing rain eventually reached a point of stopping. My head stopped dripping after a while, but I had no idea how long I stood underneath those pines; must have been an hour or two. I had no watch or phone, and the sun was hidden all day, so the seconds, minutes, and hours all blended into one massive moment—one day. I felt waterlogged and saturated, but my trail book said Woody Gap Shelter was up ahead. So, with a heavy pack shouldered, I pushed on.

I hung all my wet clothes from the rafters of the shelter. My sleeping bag was dry on the inside but damp on the outside. I felt like a caterpillar wrapped in its chrysalis when I slid into it. After a dinner of white rice and dry granola, I sat watching the water drip from my clothes onto the hardwood floor of the shelter. The floor was solid and dark, and it was carved with the names of other hikers who came before me. "Sandman 14" was at my feet. "Moon Daddy was here" was beside that. "Nomad 17" was written with a sharpie, but the black ink was starting to fade on that one.

There were so many names carved and written in that wood, and they all prompted me to pull out my knife and do the same. "Bird walks on" is what I etched into the wood.

I ate dried apricots and rubbed my tender heels. I looked through the shelter logbook and saw that Radar and Speedy were the last northbound hikers to sign in. They were a day or two ahead of me, and somewhere deep within, my competitive nature took over and gave me a target to aim for. I would catch up to them and I would pass them. I would also catch up to Leif and Chillkoot, who were only three or four days ahead. Leif wrote in the logbook about stopping in the town of Suches, Georgia for groceries and a hotel room. "I'm wet, and I need a bed!" he wrote. Junebug, Fargo, Squirrel, Violet, and Blue were all recent entries in the book. Mr. B, Jellybean, Old Smoky, Chapman, Billy Goat, Saluki, Red Dog, Spirit, and Shenandoah were all northbound hikers, and they were all within a week or two of me. I would catch them, all of them.

I brewed coffee and listened to the wind whistle through the trees. The gray sky was darkening, and I had mixed feelings about the upcoming night. I still watched my clothes drip from the rafters into puddles on the floor, and I wondered if my long sleeves would be dry come morning. Four seconds between drips, I counted. Later, it was six seconds between drips, and the newly formed puddles on the shelter floor were the only tangible things keeping me in the moment. Seven seconds passed between drips, and the puddles eventually stopped spreading. Eight seconds between drips, and I started seeing those drips as tears. There were nine seconds between teary drips, and somehow each one of those drips started to take on a distant memory.

Somehow those teardrop drips became the pieces of a much larger puzzle, now wet on the floor in front of me, and the darkening sky around me soon took away my own reflection within those puddles. The darkness settled in. Ten seconds between drips somehow turned into twenty minutes of reflection, and the blackness of the woods that night had me listening for when the next teardrop would fall. But the darkness within all those moments came to me and sucked me in, and I became lost in the darkness of that night.

And there she was, right in front of me. Her memory became the only puddle on the floor in my mind. She was the one girlfriend from my past that I truly loved, the only one, and with each drip that dropped that night, I was forced to recognize and feel that relationship all over again. Each drip represented a time and a place with that girl, and each drop forced me to relive all those memories again.

We were in high school together when she moved away without telling me. She didn't tell anyone. She simply vanished. It wasn't until later, much later, that she called to tell me she had moved away to give birth to our child. "His name is Jimmy," she told me, "and I gave him up for adoption the moment he was born."

"You did what?" I said.

"He's being raised by a good family," she said, "and the only way you'll ever get to meet him is if he comes looking for you. You can't go looking for him," she said.

I couldn't say anything. I became numb—numb to the absolute hatred I would soon feel for her and numb to the tears I would soon drop myself.

"I'm sorry," she admitted softly.

"Sorry!" I said. "You say you're sorry! I can't fucking believe what you're telling me right now, and you say you're sorry!"

"Well, I…."

"Wait just a minute," I said. "How dare you call me up like this! I mean, it's been a long fucking time since I've talked to you, and now you're calling me up with, 'Oh, hi. Just wanted to say you've got a son out there in the world.' You've got some kind of nerve calling me like this, you know that? Who the fuck do you think you are?"

"I thought you should know," she said.

"You thought I should know!"

"Yeah," she said.

"What happened to you telling me when you were pregnant?" I said. "What happened to that?"

"I know you're angry," she said, "and I don't blame you for anything."

"Damn right, I'm angry!"

"I couldn't tell you back then," she said. "I just couldn't. You know how bad things got when we were together in high school, and how do you think I feel now calling you up like this? I hate it! It rips me apart. And I'm truly sorry that I didn't tell you back then, I really am, but I'm telling you now, and that's the best I can do."

"Are you sure it's mine?" I asked.

There was a pause. "Yes, I'm sure," she said. "Listen, I'm not calling you now to beg for your forgiveness or anything like that. I'm calling you now because too much time has passed, and you deserve to know the truth."

"Well, I can't help but fuckin' hate you right now, and I can't even think about forgiveness... And honestly, I wish you never called. Fuck you," I said as I hung up the phone.

I sat there for a long time, wondering if she'd call me back. She didn't. I could taste the anger and hatred that sat with me. I couldn't get that taste out of my mouth. Waves of guilt and shame came over me that I couldn't stop.

A week or two later, I received a letter in the mail without a return address. I opened it to find a note and two pictures of a little boy sitting on a tricycle. The note simply said, "I'm sorry."

I felt both anger and love looking at those pictures. I saw a very young version of myself in those pictures, and the brown eyes and dimples left no doubt I was looking at my blood. The sadness made it hard for me to breathe, and the only thing I could do was smoke. I pulled the lighter from my pocket, lit my cigarette, and then I burned those pictures in my ashtray. I watched them bubble and burn with green and blue flames, but I looked at each of those pictures long enough to burn the image of that boy into my brain. The guilt and the shame never burned away though, and I drank vodka to numb myself, just like my father used to do. I couldn't drink fast enough to escape it all because those dimples on his cheeks were just like mine.

I sat in the corner of Woody Gap Shelter with my knees pulled close to my chest. I created my own warmth in the synthetic sleeping bag, and I smoked quietly with the soft rain still falling. My mother used to smoke quietly at our kitchen table late at night, and she would smoke one after another, hoping that the next one would quiet her nerves more than the one before. As a young teenager, I would sneak out of bed at night and watch my mother in the kitchen as she sorted through her stack of unpaid bills. The look on her face during those nights is still etched into my brain, and I can still hear her whispering to herself, "Five dollars toward this… Ten dollars toward that." There was never enough money to pay the bills in full, but there was enough to keep the lights on. The stack of bills got higher as we got taller, and my mother kept smoking quietly late at night come the end of the month.

I pulled the second-to-last cigarette from my pack, and I inhaled the smoky sounds of the mountains at night. My eyes were heavy with exhaustion, so I dropped my head onto the hardwood floor of the shelter to rest.

Our mother was furious when she found out about little Jimmy being adopted. "How could that happen without us knowing about it?" she said. Andy told her the truth about what happened because he thought it was the right thing to do, but she was beside herself, pacing the floor. She was bullshit at Andy too, telling him he was so much like our father. Then Andy got pissed, and that was the argument that caused him to leave for good.

When our father died, the whole family gathered to watch his children throw his ashes into the ocean. I can still see the tears rolling down my sister's face as she poured the ashes out of the bag, and I can still hear my grandmother talking about how unfair it was that she outlived one of her own children. That was the last time I saw Andy alive.

3

The morning arrived with gray cemetery skies and rodents and birds that scurried about the earth in their search for food. Maybe they were searching for an early spring lover? I don't know about them, but I sure was missing my lover. I felt anxious and vulnerable that morning as my oatmeal warmed on my stove, and I wanted to get moving. I patched my tender heels with rubber mole skin, and I patched the memories of my son and his mother with the hopes that the clouds would soon clear up. I needed the sun to shine, and I needed more cigarettes.

I wondered if Jada would wait six months for me to return. I wondered if Robert would check in on her from time to time. I wondered if I would make it all the way to Maine.

State Road 60 intersected the trail at the town of Suches, Georgia, and the town had a population under two hundred. Tritt's Grocery Store and a closet-sized post office made up that town as far as I could see—it was hardly a dot on the map. *Welcome to Suches!* I thought. *The smallest town in the history of towns!*

Tritt's, however, sold cigarettes, snuff, dip, chew, cigars, pipe tobacco, vape juice, and rolling papers—I felt like buying one of everything. The entire back wall of the store was covered in tobacco products, and I wanted that wall all to myself. It was beautiful! There was an old-school pay phone in the corner of Tritt's too, and I wondered if it still worked. Maybe I could call Jada. A twenty-something-year-old southern boy sat on a bar stool behind the counter and shook his head at me in my damp clothes. The corners of his mouth were stained brown with dried tobacco juice, and he rubbed his nose and grunted something strange as I put cheese, crackers, water, peanut butter, prunes, bread, bananas and a carton of Marlboro Reds on the counter.

"You'z smokin' out thea?" he asked.

"Excuse me?" I said.

He grunted again. "Are ya smokin' out there on da trail?"

"Ah, yeah," I said.

"Ya know, you'z'd be betta off chewin' on diss!" he said, grinning. His teeth were dirty brown, and I could see the finely cut chew wedged between his teeth and gums.

"Yeah, probably," I said. "I think I'll stick with the smokes though."

"You'z goin' all da way?"

"To Maine?" I said. "Yeah, I'm headed to Maine."

"Never did understand you'z hikin' boyz," he said. "Why in de hell would you'z walk dat far?"

My mouth opened, as if I were ready to explain all my intellectual reasons for hiking over two thousand miles, but then I stopped and looked at who I was explaining myself to. I simply said, "I dunno, man. Seems like the right thing to do."

"Hmm… Well, God blessya," he said, shaking his head again. "You'z still be betta off chewing on tobacca out thea."

"Yep, you're probably right," I said.

I paid for my supplies and asked if the pay phone in the corner still worked. He gave me the nod, and I asked for a couple of dollars in quarters. I pumped the coins into the slot and dialed Jada's number. When she answered, I could tell from her scratchy voice that I woke her up. Her tone was playful and excited though, which made me smile into the receiver—she didn't seem pissed that I wasn't there.

"Do you miss me?" she asked.

I paused. Should I tell her I missed her? Should I tell her how friggin' cold it was? Should I confess to her that I felt like I made a tremendous mistake by coming to the woods? Should I tell her about my split heels and how it rained ninety percent of the time? Should I tell her about the permanent stains on the mouth of the southern boy on the stool who was watching me on the pay phone? I breathed deeply, "Of course I miss you, baby."

"Where are you now?" she asked.

"Suches, Georgia," I said, as I raised my eyebrows toward the redneck boy, now leaning backward on his stool. "Population under two hundred," I said in a whisper.

"Is that even considered a town?" she said, laughing.

After fifteen minutes of mostly me talking, I could tell she was hiding some of her feelings. She didn't talk about what was really on her mind, so I eventually lied to her, saying that I had to get going. She sighed deeply into the phone, and I promised her another phone call the next time I reached town.

The young redneck on the stool spit brown juice into a coffee cup on the counter and wished me luck as I packed away my supplies and hoisted my pack. I walked across the street to the post office only to see the "Out to Lunch" sign hanging on the front door. I wanted to fill out a couple of postcards for her and Robert and mail them, but apparently, I had to wait on that. I took off my pack, dropped it on the sidewalk, and sat on it. I was excited to have cheese, smokes, and prunes, so I sat there in front of the post office wondering about the rest of the day. I smoked a cigarette and ate cheese. The door across the street at Tritt's swung open, and the redneck cowboy from the stool stuck his head out the front door to tell me that Bob would be by within the hour to take me to the cabins if I wanted.

I lifted my shoulders. "Cabins? Who's Bob?" I shouted.

"Bob's the taxi man," he said. "If you'z wonna sleep in a real bed tonight and take a hot showa, then Bob will be along within the hour to take ya. He drives a big blue pickup, can't miss'm."

"How much for a cabin?" I asked.

"I dunno, maybe thirty," he said. "A couple other hikers got a ride yesterday, and wit dis rain on da way, maybe they'll stay another night and split da fee witchya."

"Okay, buddy. Thanks."

"You betchya," he said, with a grin and a long, dark spit onto the sidewalk.

Time stood still on the side of the road as I sat on my pack. I wanted to fill out a postcard to Jada, but like the sign on the door said, I was *out to lunch* with my thoughts. I was wet and heavy from rainwater, and the sky was a timeless shade of gray. I wanted to feel dry and warm. I wanted the sun. I recalled the warm fire at the Amicalola Falls cabin, and I craved that warmth. I felt like writing, but I didn't feel like fishing for my journal in my pack. The cheese tasted creamy, and my smoke made everything seem okay. I felt reassured knowing I had a new lighter and a carton of smokes to last me.

It was a faint sound at first, but I could hear it climbing up some big hill in the distance. It was the hum of a battered engine that needed help, and the sound grew louder and louder as the engine got closer. I wondered if it was Bob's taxi service headed my way.

Then, suddenly, I was reliving some of my teenage days again, where me, my brother, and the boys from our neighborhood would drink beer in the afternoon at my mother's kitchen table. We used to skip school and drink beer there in the middle of the day, and around 5:30 we'd start listening for the distant hum of my mother's engine coming up the street. The Volkswagen hatchback she used to drive was so old and beat up, and it desperately needed a new muffler, but my brother and I were never embarrassed or ashamed of our mother driving a car with a coat hanger holding up the muffler, because it gave us a chance to drink in the warmth and comfort of the kitchen. That car was so fucking loud though, and we could always hear her coming from at least a mile away. Every school-day-drinking episode always started with a loving phone call to my mother's work to make sure she wasn't coming home early, and to ask if we should pull any meat out of the freezer for dinner. And we never played any music in the kitchen after 5:15 because we needed to be able to hear that engine of hers coming. And right around the fourth or fifth, sometimes sixth beer, someone would say, "Shh! Shh!" and everyone would listen in like hound dogs before confirming, "Yep, that's her. Let's go! Let's go! Let's go! Let's get everything cleaned up and get outta here. We've got ninety seconds before she reaches the driveway. Come on, let's go!"

And down the back stairs everyone would go, as I pushed in all the chairs around the table and my brother wiped everything down. We'd make sure the ashtrays were empty and the condensation rings were wiped clean from the table before we'd look around the room one last time and kill the lights. We'd leave that kitchen just like we found it, and once everyone was out of the house, we'd run through the backyards and across neighborhood streets to the nearby woods by the train tracks where we would all laugh and howl and raise our beer cans to not getting caught yet again. Every afternoon drinking session would start in the warmth and comfort of our mother's kitchen, but it would always end in the backwoods near the train tracks just west of our neighborhood. "Thank God for that piece of shit Volkswagen!" we'd say. That car with the shitty muffler saved our asses every time we drank at our mother's kitchen table...

"You looking for a ride up to the cabins?" said the voice that woke me from my roadside daydream.

"You Bob?" I asked.

"Yeah, you need a ride?"

"How much?" I asked.

"Seven."

"Will you take five?"

"Nope. I'll take seven though."

"Ok," I said. "Seven it is."

Bob's blue pickup truck roared through the hillside town of Suches with a screaming horsepower engine that scared the hell out of all the black birds in the nearby trees. The Grateful Dead's *Sugar Magnolia* pumped through his speakers, and Bob tapped his eighty-plus-year-old fingers on the steering wheel as he drove. The volume of the music was louder than his battered engine, and he drove the curvy roads of Georgia at ridiculous speeds. It was obvious that Bob was a regular at Tritt's because of all the various tobacco products that were littered inside his truck. He had a carton of Winstons on the dashboard and a few empty packs of Marlboro Greens on the floor. Crumpled up bags of Red Man tobacco and empty tins of Copenhagen snuff were in the center console, and the cup holder held his spit cup, which was nearly full. Every time Bob turned a corner at fifty or so miles an hour, the thick black juice in the cup would come close to spilling over.

Bob had a red bandana tied around his neck, like the one we used to tie around our cocker spaniel as kids, and his wire-brush white hair hadn't seen a wash in quite some time. He wore brand new Wrangler blue jeans though, and a checkerboard shirt cuffed at the wrist. I remember wishing my friends were there to see the size of the Confederate flag belt buckle he had on because it must have weighed at least two pounds. And I knew that buckle was custom-made because it had *BOB* etched across the bottom of it. He was obviously proud of that two-pound piece of metal that kept his stomach from falling forward even further.

"So, Bob," I finally said. "You've been in Georgia a while?"

"All my life," he said.

I opted not to tell him I was a Bostonian, and I couldn't think of anything else I really wanted to know about Bob, so I held onto my seatbelt as he continued to roar through the hills. One more sharp turn before Bob locked the brakes and stopped in front of a dirt driveway.

"Cabins are down there," he said. "That'll be seven dollars, my boy." I paid the man and shouldered my pack before thanking him for the ride. Bob lit a cigarette and used the bandana around his neck to wipe his nose. "Safe travels," he said, before hitting the gas and storming off down the road.

I stood on the side of that Georgia road for a few minutes as I looked down the dirt driveway that coiled around a series of pine trees. I couldn't see any cabins, but I could see the remains of an old flatbed trailer with deflated tires and a broken axle. A handmade sign was in front of the trailer, and in orange lettering, the sign said, *Blue Ridge Cabins! Hikers Are Welcome!*

I walked the dirt driveway a quarter mile before I arrived at the front desk where some dark-skinned Native American guy told me that I was 'very, very lucky today' because he only had one room left and it was mine if I wanted it.

"How much?" I asked.

"Forty-two dollars," he said.

"Forty-two?" I said. "Any chance I could pitch my tent somewhere outside?"

"Sure," he said. "That'll be twelve dollars and no shower."

I knew I didn't need any extra time to think about it, but I paused and looked around the place, as if to suggest the price for the room was a little high. I was hoping he'd offer me a reduced rate or something, maybe a free breakfast, but after a moment or two of silence, I ended my little standoff by telling him I'd take the room.

"Perfect!" he said.

"How many beds are in a room?" I asked.

"Two," he said.

"Well, if any other hikers come around looking for a bed, could you send them my way?"

"Oh, yes sir," said the Native guy, but I could tell by the look on his face that there wouldn't be any other hikers sharing the room with me.

I tied a long piece of rope from one curtain rod over the bed to the bathroom door handle on the other side of the room, then back to the curtain rod over the other bed. I hung everything I had up to dry on my zig-zag clothesline, and I took a long, hot shower. I thought about all the work I had to do just to dry my clothes, and I immediately felt grateful for the washer and dryer I had in my Florida apartment. The warm water in that shower felt more refreshing than any shower I could remember, and my teeth felt squeakier than usual after brushing.

I crawled into bed, excited for the soft sheets, and I blew smoke rings as I laid there. The sheets of cotton felt like silk. I smoked. I ate cheese and peanut butter crackers. I smoked more. I smoked in bed like a man I once knew. I scratched my incoming beard like a man I once knew. I scratched my balls like he used to scratch his. I smoked again. Then I wondered about where that man was during that moment? Could he somehow see me in that cabin? In that bed?

I recalled a few of the stories he used to tell me as a kid at bedtime. He was a good storyteller, sometimes. And then I looked at the strange cabin walls surrounding me, and I couldn't help but think of him as a stranger too. I thought about how I once loved that man, but then how I grew to hate him. My eyes were far from sleeping that night, and I smoked in the dark space of that room, recalling the times he used to come home drunk. I recalled the times he used to sit in his car in the parking lot, drinking, while I played in my Little League baseball games. I thought of all the times he honked his horn when I'd get a hit or stole a base. I could still taste the humiliation and embarrassment I felt on the day he decided to come and sit with all the other parents on the bleachers. Why couldn't he be like the other fathers in our town? Why did he have to be the town drunk? Why did everyone shake their heads at him when he came around? Truth be told, I knew why everyone looked down on him— they all knew he was a drunk. And somewhere deep down inside, I always knew he'd never change. He was the man that stabbed me with a fishhook just to show me how the pain wasn't all that bad. Then, when I cried, he called me a pussy and told me to grow up. He was the man who had affairs with other women. He was the man who cheated on everything and didn't pay child support. He was the deadbeat man that everyone knew about. He was the man that I felt ashamed of.

And there I was, alone in a cabin in Suches, Georgia, thinking about my father. I was frightened by the thought of how much I was like him. I felt scared, lost, and angry that I spent forty-two dollars on a cabin room that made me feel like the man I'd grown to hate.

5:08pm

Our father walked out on us when we were old enough to realize he wasn't coming back. My brother acted like he was relieved, but my sister was angry and sad. Our mother was scared, and she would cry at night after she thought everyone was sleeping. Mother took a second job to keep food on the table, and she was worried that we had too much freedom as kids. She was afraid of our rebellion, and naturally, it came. The welfare she had for her children came in the form of food stamps from the state, and we grew tired of that, especially my brother. Our father sent each of us a Christmas card one year with a twenty-dollar bill on the inside, and he wrote something about Santa Clause and missing us and Ho-Ho-Ho! Andy gave his twenty bucks to our mother.

4

I woke up the next morning in a pool of sweat because the heater on the wall of the cabin never shut off. One hundred degrees never felt so good. I could hear voices outside the cabin door, and the sunbeams through the gaps in the window curtains illuminated those spaces in the room. That same space was so dark just hours before, but in the morning, it looked new, fresh, and warm. It was eight o'clock, and my clothes were crisp and dry on the clothesline. I sat on the edge of the bed eating crackers and dry oatmeal straight from the package. I took another shower for the sake of having spent forty-two dollars on the water, and my body felt sleek as I got dressed. I went through my backpack and decided to leave behind certain items that I wouldn't be using every day. I left a book of Poe's short stories on the dresser that I wasn't reading, and I left my small fishing pole and mini tackle box next to the bed I slept in. I downsized from four shirts to three, from three pairs of socks to two. I only needed one fork and spoon, so I left my backups on the bed. I didn't need two plates, so I only kept one. I went through everything, and if it wasn't absolutely necessary, I left it behind. Every ounce and every pound mattered because, if I had to carry it on my back all day, then everything mattered.

There were several hikers congregating outside my cabin on a small grassy courtyard area when I left my room. Some of them sat at a picnic table eating and talking, while others stretched their legs and double-checked their gear. I walked over and introduced myself to Radar and Speedy, Mr. B and Chillkoot, Junebug and Squirrel, and Fargo and Leif. They all seemed happy enough, but they were looking around as if waiting for the first hiker to leave the courtyard so everyone else could follow.

And that's when the adrenaline and my competitive nature really struck. Suddenly, I saw myself as a thoroughbred horse on racing day, like I was in the Kentucky Derby or something, and I was just waiting for my jockey to kick me in the side to send me on my way. There I was, standing among all those other hikers, those other horses, and we all seemed to be strapping ourselves into the starting gate for the upcoming race. I could hear the imaginary fans in the stands and those men with their silly hats and horns, as they blew out that lovely tune announcing the beginning of the big race. It was like the Appalachian Derby in my head—the longest hiker race known to man! It was the 2,192 mile hiker race, and everyone was getting ready for some racing that morning.

Annnnnnd… they're off! And Junebug takes the early lead with huge strides of twenty-five miles a day, and Chillkoot hangs in second with a near twenty, and Radar slips to the back of the pack, and the field begins to spread itself out, and here comes the first turn, and *Oh!* there's a spill, and there's a horse stopping for lunch, and Squirrel and Fargo are beginning to pick up the pace, and Leif looks like he's slowing down, and Speedy is anything but, and the oldest horse of the day, Mr. B., is hanging around! Yes sir, he's hanging around! And it's gonna be a close one! It's gonna be close, but you've got plenty of time for lunch and dinner several times over because it's the longest hiker race there is, and not every hiker makes it. Welcome to the Appalachian Derby, everyone! It's the longest hiker race there is.

I laughed at my silly and childish thoughts, but I gotta say it felt pretty good to recognize I was smiling. And I wanted more of that—more smiling. The hikers that surrounded me seemed easygoing and friendly with smiles on their faces, and a part of me wanted to get to know them and hike with them. I wanted to take it easy like them. But the other part of me wanted to leave them in my dust and never see them again.

I've always been competitive like that. As a kid, I spent my time thinking about how I could run faster than you, lift more weight than you, talk cooler than you, drive faster than you, get the prettier girl before you, drink more than you— there was always the ambitious pride of wanting to be better than you. There was always the ego-inflating comfort in knowing I would eventually beat you. I *needed* to be better than you, and I worked hard at that. I *needed* to be noticed by you, and I worked hard at that too. The pursuit of winning always kept me going because losing just wasn't an option. It was never the car that won the race, it was always the driver. Back in high school, I would gain ten pounds in one sitting just to drink you under the table. Then, I would puke everything up and keep going because if I stopped, you would have the chance to catch me. And that was never going to happen. It was never about being part of the team. Sure, I was a part of a lot of different teams, be it football, baseball, or basketball, but teamwork didn't mean much of anything to me. Not only did I have to beat my opponent, but I also had to beat my teammates. I had to outlast them and outperform them. And if my coaches weren't giving me the game ball after every game, then something was wrong on my inside. If I wasn't praised first in the local newspaper, then I'd practice harder, work harder, and sweat more. And I'd do it until they did recognize me—until they did say my name first in the paper. Whether it was the football field, the baseball diamond, or the hiker race of the Appalachian Derby; whether it was the girl, the beer, or the trail I hiked, I always felt the need to be first. I *needed* to be first to that summit, because then, I could sit back and smoke my Marlboro with the satisfaction of knowing that I beat them, all of them.

"Hey, how's it going?" he said. "My name is Leif, and this here's Radar. Haven't seen you out here yet; what's your trail name?"

"Bird," I said.

"Nice to meet you, Bird. You must've pulled in after us yesterday."

"Yeah," I said. "I got here sometime in the afternoon."

Leif kept talking about himself and his hike and his reasons for being in the woods. He seemed nice and all, but his reasons for hiking were different than mine.

"Isn't this great?" he said. "Don't you just love being out here in nature like this?"

I had a feeling that I would spend more time with Leif and the other hikers further down the trail, but in that moment, I viewed Leif and everyone else as my competitors. My focus that day wasn't on making friends, it was on whether I'd beat them to the finish line or not. If they hiked twelve miles in a day, I'd hike fifteen. If they stopped hiking each day at five in the afternoon, then I'd hike until seven. If they went three hours without water, I'd go four. If they ate two packages of chicken for dinner, I'd eat three. And since it was the longest hiker race known to man, I purposefully sat on my pack that morning outside those cabins, waiting until each and every hiker left, because that way, I'd get to enjoy all the benefits of passing each and every one of them along the trail.

I could see myself gaining on each one of them and closing the gap. I could see myself getting right up behind them, then passing them, and the thought of them looking at my backside as I widened the gap between us—that's what drove me. Leif might have been out in the woods to take in Mother Nature and the Zen of it all, but I was out in those woods to compete against him. Losing to him just wasn't an option.

And maybe those competitive thoughts and feelings stem back to watching my mother at our kitchen table with all those bills stacked up in front of her? Maybe those thoughts stem from my father leaving when I was only eleven? I mean, I can still hear my mother crying for Christ's sake, and I can still remember her asking me if I could handle being the man around the house after he left. I remember the hatred I felt. The anger. "Yeah," I said. "I'm ready. I can be the man around here."

And from that moment on, I was no longer a kid. I no longer took orders from anyone. I no longer viewed myself as that scared little kid, running and hiding in the bushes in the rain when daddy came home all shitfaced. From that moment on, I had to be stronger. I had to be the man my younger brother and sister could lean on. I had to be a better man than the man who left us behind. I had to beat my old man at being a man, and I set my mind on that.

"Yeah," I told my mother. "I'm ready to be the man of the house."

Maybe I am who I am because of all those things that happened when I was a kid? Who knows? Maybe it did stem back to my father and his drinking days. Maybe it did stem back to the day Susie told me about my son. Maybe it did stem back to my sad and bitchy sister and my confused little brother. Maybe it stemmed back to puberty and my mother trying to tell me about sex and the *love* between a man and a woman. Maybe it stemmed back to all the memories I have of the kids in our neighborhood playing ball with their fathers when my father wasn't around anymore. I hated that! Maybe it was all that shit.

All I knew was that Rock and Little Rock left an impression on me, and it was something that stuck. It was refreshing to meet a father and his son like that, and maybe I was like Little Rock in some ways. Maybe I got caught up in thinking about how my father wasn't the Rock I wanted him to be. Who knows? Either way, the truth is that I sat on my pack that morning outside those cabins and I waited until every last hiker left that courtyard, and I did it because of the fucked-up sense of pride I've got. I waited until each and every one of them got a good head start, and then I strapped on my pack with the idea that I would catch them and pass them, every last one of them. It was the longest hiker race known to man, and I'd be damned if any of them would finish before me.

The next day I woke up to the cold pitter-patter sounds of raindrops on my tent. I was damp and stiff and sore. I laid in my sleeping bag thinking about the extra weight I'd have to carry with a wet tent. I wasn't looking forward to being wet again. Blood Mountain was a steep uphill climb that day and my feet felt bloody, raw, and worn. There was a grinding pain at the back of my heels, and the added weight of my wet pack slowed me down. I hated feeling heavy and slow. My feet looked like white raisins when I stopped for a snack and a chance to change my wet socks for drier ones.

I reached the summit of Blood Mountain later that afternoon, and the shelter of three walls and a leaky roof was already full. I cursed myself for spending the majority of my day *not* trying to compete against everyone else. I was trying to *enjoy* my day in nature, like Leif suggested, rather than being in pursuit of him, but when I was forced to pitch my tent in the rain that night, those feelings came rushing back to me. I was out in the rain, yet again, because I let *them* beat me to the shelter. I was cold and wet, yet again, because I tried to *enjoy* the beauty around me rather than chase down the hikers in front of me. I told myself throughout the day *not* to think about the race I was in, but then, at the end of the day, I saw where that had gotten me! Every spot in the shelter was taken that night, and I had to plant the stakes of my tent in the wet earth, yet again, while every other hiker was snug and dry and warm and protected. All my gear got soaked, yet again, and I felt angry and bitter.

Fuck them, I said to myself. The beauty and tranquility that Leif spoke of in nature might be good for him, but that was not me, and I fell asleep in my wet tent that night with the idea of leaving him and his bullshit ideas of beauty in my dust. And boy, oh boy, that competitiveness was back, thicker than ever… but then I realized it never really went away in the first place.

Neel's Gap, Georgia, had an outfitter store at the intersection of the trail with a paved road, and that's where I saw the first signs of civilian life other than belt-buckle Bob and the dip-sucking southern cowboy at Tritt's tobacco store. I saw a younger girl and an older woman behind the counter of that outfitter store, selling Ramen noodles, granola bars, Gatorade, aspirin, and trail mix to all the hikers. I saw rows and rows of shelves stocked with all the things that a hiker might dream about having. They had Gillette razors for those with scratchy faces and overpriced Patagonia shirts with long sleeves. They had hiking boots, walking sticks, and maps of each section of the trail. I dropped my pack near the front door of the store, and I stared at all the baked goods they had in a display case. I wanted one of everything, and I had the urge to hire the pretty brown-haired girl behind the counter to help me eat it all. She was young and beautiful, and I was missing Jada. So, I purchased an everything bagel with cream cheese and coffee with real cream, and I smiled at the southern accent of the young cashier as she handed me back my change. "Have a nice day now," she said.

I laughed at the sight of one hiker trying to ship his acoustic guitar back home to New Jersey. I mean, what was he thinking? Was he really gonna carry that thing over two thousand miles just so he could play a couple of songs every night? Romantic in a way, I guess, but come on, man! It brought a smile to my face watching that guy say goodbye to his guitar.

There were two stacks of cardboard boxes in the corner of that outfitter store with hiker's names on them. They were food drops that those hikers had sent to themselves, and Radar stuffed his face as he sat in the corner with his food box in front of him. He had a Milky Way in one hand and a fistful of dried apricots in the other. "This is awesome!" he said. "Food never tasted so good."

Radar was a thin, tall guy, and it looked like he'd fall over backwards when he stood up and put his pack on. The pack was two times thicker than he was! He had pale white skin and a splotchy beard that wasn't really growing in well, and I overheard him telling Junebug that he took his trail name from the character Radar on the TV show M*A*S*H. The hiker, Radar, was a goofy, awkward-looking guy, and his eyes were too close together on his face, so he looked just like the guy from that TV show! I thought it was clever that he gave himself that name—Radar was a good fit for him.

At first, I just ordered a refill of coffee from my young new friend behind the counter. I loved the way she smiled and said, "You're welcome" when I thanked her for the coffee. Her smile had me returning to that same counter line five minutes later for a granola bar. "That'll be two dollars," she said. *Oh, yes it will* I thought. And then, eight minutes later, I was back in her line buying a twenty-ounce *Very Fine* orange juice, and once again, I thanked her for the fabulous customer service. Within forty-five minutes, I purchased a new long-sleeved Patagonia shirt, a post card, a block of cheese, Pop-Tarts, another post card, and two pairs of thick wool socks. I purchased all those items at different times and all from her line.

"That'll be $55.95 please."

"That'll be $2 please."

"That'll be $3.95."

"$5.25 please."

"75 cents."

"$18 please."

And after every single purchase, she just smiled and tilted her head to the left and said, "Thank you."

Of course, she knew I was playing with her like that. Of course, she knew I thought she was beautiful. Of course, she knew it would be a long time before I saw someone as beautiful as she was. And, of course, she knew I was thankful for her playing along. Of course, she knew I was missing Jada.

There were people on vacation and families with kids at Neel's Gap that day. There were section hikers and weekend hikers and fathers and sons at Neel's Gap too, and you could easily tell the difference between the thru-hikers and everyone else because of how dirty and gritty they were. The lower legs of the other hikers weren't covered in mud like the thru-hikers, and their hair wasn't crusty and nappy. They had clean faces, and they were probably the hikers who liked to stand in front of mirrors with all their gear on so they could view themselves as hikers, if only for a moment. It's comical really, when you think about it, and I picked the dirt from underneath my fingernails as I sat on the floor watching all of them buy their stuff. It was impossible not to notice the excitement in the eyes of all the weekend hikers though. They had that extra pep in their step because they were being adventurous and active for a change. They had that excitement in their eyes, you know, the look that said, *we're so excited because we're going for a hike in nature and we're being good to ourselves!*

Watching those people was entertaining, but I was more interested in finding out what the weather looked like for the upcoming days. The rain had been super harsh on me up to that point, and I felt just fine sitting in the dry corner of that outfitter store watching my young brown-haired beauty behind the counter in her thick ski sweater.

The local newspaper promised chilly but sunny days to come, and that thought made me want to write a poem. I needed the sun, and I needed to dry my feet out. Out from the back room of the store walked a different woman, maybe sixty years old, possibly the owner of the place, and she carried a sign in her hands that she hung on the front door. I peeled myself off the floor and walked over to it. It read:

So far, 50% of thru-hikers have gone home due to the harsh weather conditions. This information is provided by the Appalachian Trail Headquarters. High temperature today is 38. Low temperature tonight is 15. Forecast for tomorrow is partially sunny and cold, with more rain. If you're hiking on, you'd better stock up here!

Thanks,
Management

I stepped back from the sign in disbelief. *Fifty percent,* I thought. I looked over at Chillkoot and Leif, Radar and Mr. B, and I thought about us as the remaining fifty percent—I felt proud to be a part of that number. But then I felt embarrassed for the other fifty percent, who I never met, because they had already gone home, after only one week on the trail. I mean, come on! They planned for this trip, they trained for this trip, they spent money on this trip, they told their friends and family about this trip, and then, after one week of a six-month hike, they quit and went home. *What phonies!*

I thought about those fifty percent phonies for a while. I tried to feel some empathy for them, but I couldn't. Simply put, they were quitters. They were too weak and thin-skinned, and they *should* feel embarrassed about their effort. They were the losers and the phonies—they were the other fifty percent.

Then it was back again, very strong, that competitive urge, and it just took over. But this time, my competitiveness had more ego tied to it, because who in their right mind would quit after only a week? What would everyone say to me if I quit after only a week? What would Robert say? I thought about how I'd walk home in shame, tail between my legs, and I thought about how others would talk down on me. "I knew he wouldn't make it," they'd say. And that thought fueled me like nothing else. I no longer cared about the rain or the rips in the backs of my heels. I no longer cared about the mountains I'd have to climb or the cold nights in a damp sleeping bag. All I cared about was finishing what I started because, what kind of man would I be if I didn't finish? What kind of man would I be if I cashed everything in after only one week?

I decided not to call Jada from the phone outside the store in Neel's Gap. I had a long uphill climb ahead of me, and I was sure she'd bring me down with the depressive tones in her voice about how she missed me. So, I tipped my imaginary cap one last time to my southern counter girl, and I headed out to climb that mountain. I was glad to have the memory of that counter girl smiling back at me after I bought nearly one of everything in the store.

My new Patagonia shirt felt silky and smooth, and the new socks added cushion to the back of my heels. I felt like a new hiker, warm and ready to climb. Leif had left the outfitter store a few minutes before I did, so I set my sights on catching him and taking his spot in the shelter that night. The noise from the people in the store and the traffic sounds from the paved road soon faded away, as I climbed the twisting trail upward. The sounds of nothing in the forest became loud again. The climb was gradual, but steep and rocky in parts. At times, my breathing got heavy, and I didn't like hiking with a full belly and a backpack full of supplies.

Then I heard it. Just as I rounded a curve in the trail, I could hear the snap of a twig and the rustling of leaves off to my left. I stopped in my tracks and turned that way. My heart rate quickened as I scanned the woods around me. I had never seen a bear before, and I didn't want that moment to be my first. *Come on, come on* I said under my breath, *show yourself.* Then, another snap, and my eyes turned quickly to zoom in, and that's when I saw it, nearly two hundred feet away. That's when I saw Leif leaning against a pine tree to take a crap. And *oh!* how I wish it were a bear or a fox or an elephant or a train or a bus full of old ladies! Oh, how I wished it were anything other than the sight of Leif's squatting ass.

My brother and I were always competing against one another as kids. Whether it was street hockey, soccer, baseball, or football, we always had to beat one another. I always viewed it as a healthy form of competition between brothers, but it obviously wasn't that way for Andy. I never linked my competitive nature to my father, nor did I ever feel a need to be a better man than my father was. I wasn't the oldest son, and my mother never asked me to be the man around the house, so it saddens me to read about how my brother put that type of pressure on himself. He never talked to me about that.

5

It was an hour's climb straight up to the heavens, and many of the weekend hikers elected to take the alternate blue blaze trail around the base of Wildcat Mountain. The rule of thumb is that thru-hikers stay on the white blaze trail because that *is* the Appalachian Trail. The intersecting blue blaze trails are *not* the Appalachian Trail, and it's against the so-called rules for thru-hikers to use the alternate blue blaze because they tend to be easier and less demanding. Sure, any hiker could use those trails, but if you were a thru-hiker and someone saw you on the blue blaze, then your commitment to the Appalachian Trail would be called into question. I never read that anywhere, but that was the unwritten rule. And I didn't want anyone, especially Radar and Leif, looking at me as if I was someone willing to cut corners like that.

The store at Neel's Gap and the people there reminded me of just how quiet the woods can be. Without people around, the conversations throughout the day took place between my ears. Without the chatter of people and the smiles from beautiful counter girls giving me back my change, the world can get really quiet. Without all the city buildings and transit buses, the world goes silent in the woods. Without all the traffic signals, beeping car horns, electric bicycles, jelly donut eating fat cops, bill collectors on the telephone, *ring-ring,* the world can get frightfully quiet. The wilderness grows silent when all those distractions are no longer there, and that's when the conversation between the ears really starts to make noise.

The wilderness is mossy and moist with gray stones everywhere. Some stones are sharp, yet others are smooth. Were the smooth stones once sharp? My guess was yes, and I thought about the amount of time it would take to smooth out all those jagged edges. It would take years and years of pounding weather and harsh storms to smooth all that out, and somehow, I saw myself in all those sharp rocks—I knew I was sharp and jagged just like they were. Yet, I admired the soft round surface of the smooth stones, and I wanted to be more like those instead. Sometimes I talked to myself out loud, wondering if the pounding rain would slowly change me from jagged to smooth? I was attracted to the smooth, round surface of those stones.

The silent wilderness gets interrupted sometimes with woodpeckers pecking at the bark, but I rarely saw them. The wind often invades the wilderness with chilly bursts of air and stiff breezes that bring about shivering, but I could never predict when those howling winds would happen. The wilderness was ragwort in bloom and tiny waterfalls burping through mountain faces, and I never knew when I'd see or hear the next new wild thing.

What I saw in those woods usually reflected the type of wilderness I felt inside. When I saw the baby ferns of fuzzy green new beginnings, I often felt like a kid, so small. When I saw circular dollar weeds big enough to eat off, I got hungry. When I heard the subtle sounds of far-off birds or the movements of rodents that I couldn't see, I felt startled and insecure. And all those unseen things stirred a fear of one kind or another inside—the things out of sight startled me the most.

But it was early spring, and the wilderness promised the rebirth of so many things. And as I hiked, I saw all those promises starting to come true. And as I saw them, I felt them. As I felt them, I wondered about what was coming next. *What was I promised?* I wondered. I peeled the moss from the face of a stone and smelled it. I ran my fingers over the chilly smooth green surface—I spent more time than ever thinking about such a thing—moss. I hiked on. I threw that piece of moss away as I waited for the next thing to come into sight. There was nothing to distract me from my curiosities, and I thought about the men, women, and children who once lived in those woods centuries before me. I wishfully looked for arrowheads and pottery pieces, thinking that maybe I'd find something precious, but knowing full well that if I did, it would be nothing more than random luck. I rang out the bandana from around my head, dripping sweat, which attracted small gnats I couldn't see at first. I wiped the crusty corners of my eyes with the wet bandana, and I could smell the sweat of all my work that day. The more I hiked, the more I thought. The more I thought about myself, the less I liked what I saw. The wilderness showed so much promise, but my insides were still dark and cold. I felt unbalanced on the path I walked.

Would I be able to survive in the woods with only my bare hands and the legs I walk on? If I hadn't remembered what I'd seen on TV or YouTube, would I have a clue as to how to hunt and create shelter for myself? I remembered my childhood days as a kid in the woods behind our house, and I would play in all the rocks and dirt, thinking I was a pilgrim or a pirate or an Indian. I would pretend to be someone else, from another time, and I would act out the roles that I saw on those TV shows and cartoons. As a kid, I used to love having other kids from the neighborhood play with me; but as an adult, I had no interest in hiking with others. Curious. I knew for sure that I didn't want to play pilgrims and Indians with any of the other hikers, and I had no interest in hiking all day with them only to tell campfire stories at night. Curious.

There was nothing to distract me, and I quickly grew tired of all the thoughts that spun round and round in my head. I thought about turning around and hiking back to Neel's Gap for the much-welcomed distraction of my young counter girl. The thought of drinking coffee and watching her smile seemed more than all right with me, but then I thought of Jada all alone in Florida, and I spent some time thinking about her. Did I love her? Was she the one for me? I thought about my son, and I wondered if he would ever come knocking on my door. Why wouldn't he? Why would he? I thought about my mother, my sister, and my brother, and I missed them. For the first time in a long time, I missed them.

I was the riddler without the solution to my own riddle, and I climbed those fucking rocks, one after another, with the idea that maybe, just maybe, the answers to everything would suddenly appear. And it's a curious thing too, because I wanted to hike alone, but I didn't like the thoughts that came from hiking alone.

I have never been an avid hiker. The fact is, I only hiked a handful of times before taking on the challenge of the Appalachian Trail. I hiked Blue Hills once in high school on a date, and another time when I was working for an old guy in New Hampshire. I climbed Mount Moosilauke with him, and he was nearly three times my age. I worked as his live-in butler in New Hampshire, and it was the easiest job I ever had. He was a Jewish guy with lots of money, but he was old and alone in the world. So he hired me to cook his meals, talk to him, and wash his floors twice a month. I folded his clothes along the seams and garnished his martinis with olives, and he even let me drive one of his fancy cars around town. "Treat it like it's your own," he told me. He had more money than anyone I ever knew, money handed down, and he lived in a six-bedroom house all by himself. He didn't have a wife or a lover or any kids, and I often thought about staying with him until he died. I thought about shining his shoes and washing his dirty socks until he passed away because the idea of inheriting all that money sounded pretty good at the time.

His name was Roger, and he paid me in cash every week. He dyed his hair jet black once a month and shaved every day, but the skin on his face was splotchy and weathered, like he smoked two packs of Camels a day for fifty years or something. He held his martini like a lady, with his pinky finger slightly raised, but his voice was deep and rich, like the biker dudes you see wearing leather jackets in the movies. Roger wore thick black glasses because they went well with the color of his hair, but the lenses made his eyes look twice their size. He was an interesting guy to look at because he tried to look young, but he wasn't. He was old. And he was an interesting guy to listen to because he sounded masculine, but he wasn't. He liked baby blue or pink V-neck shirts and leather boat shoes—very feminine in how he dressed, like he belonged in Florida or someplace warm.

On most weekends, I would drive back to Boston in his car and spend time with my friends and crash at my mother's place. Then, on Sunday nights, I would drive back to New Hampshire and work for him throughout the week. It was a good setup for me; a great job right out of high school, and Roger always told me how thankful he was to have me around. He was a nice guy, but a strange guy. He loved the Appalachian Trail. On days when he felt well enough, we'd drive to different sections of the trail where we'd hike around for a mile or two. He'd tell me stories of the times he hiked the trail as a younger man, and how great it was when he got to meet the other hikers.

The fact was, Roger was the one who got me interested in hiking the Appalachian Trail myself. His house in New Hampshire had a barn out back that he converted into a bar of sorts, and his house wasn't far from the trailhead, so he made it a point to welcome hikers into his home as they were passing by on the trail. He had a bunk house on top of the bar, and he let the hikers stay there for free. He was generous like that.

Besides making Roger martinis and washing his dishes, my job was to go to the post office in Glencliff each day around five to see if there were any hikers wanting to spend the night at his place. Some days there wouldn't be any hikers, but other days we'd have a packed car. It sure was a sight to see four or five hikers jammed into that little sports car of his with hiking sticks and backpacks coming out of the windows and the trunk. We were busting at the seams on those days.

And once back at the house, the hikers would sit around the bar drinking beer or vodka with Roger as they talked about their adventures on the trail. The Hiking Mommas were a team of six schoolteacher women in their late fifties, and every summer they would hike a hundred or so miles of the trail. They only had a few hundred miles of the trail left to go when I met them at Roger's place, and they were all excited at the idea of finishing the trail someday soon. It was great meeting those ladies, and I had to make two trips to the post office that day in order to get them all back to the house.

Lots of fathers and sons rolled through Roger's place, and sometimes the hiker honeymooners would stop in, but mostly it was the single hiker looking to dry out for a night or two. Everyone was always surprised at how nice the house was, and how generous Roger was. "You never know from one minute to the next what you're gonna experience," said one of the Hiking Mommas. "You never know who you're gonna meet or what kind of great place you'll run into… Like this place," she said. "This place is incredible!"

The hikers would eat and drink with Roger while he sipped his martinis, and I would run laundry through the washer and make everyone snacks. "You're the best caretaker I've ever had," Roger told me one night after everyone went to bed, "but I won't say it again," he laughed, "so that way it won't go to your head."

Saying it once was all I needed to hear though, and later that year, I decided that he was too healthy to wait around for dying. I got tired of counting down those days, and after I drank all his gin one night, I decided to take his car out for an evening mountain ride. A few hours later, Roger got a call from the Hanover police to say that a young man nearly killed himself by flipping over his car near the center of town.

I don't remember much of that night, but I do remember waking up to Roger standing over me in a hospital bed. He told me he wouldn't press changes or anything like that. But later on, a week or so after that accident, he decided to touch me on the inner thigh in that *special* kind of way, as a form of *repayment* for his totaled car and all. As I said, he was a quirky old man, but I felt like my time with him needed to come to an end. As soon as I could, I bought myself a one-way bus ticket out of that place, and I opted not to leave him a note saying goodbye.

Those memories of Roger and how I first came to know the Appalachian Trail helped push me up to the top of Tray Mountain that day, and once the climb leveled off, I was standing on the summit. I just couldn't believe it—what a sight it was to see! I spun myself around to get a full panoramic view, and not too many words can be used to describe the beauty of that place. It's the sort of place that needs to be experienced and felt, not spoken, or read about. So, I'll leave it at that. Simply magnificent.

I remember the smile that came to my face on that summit, and once again, I was aware of my smile. I was able to look back down the mountain I had just climbed, and a feeling of accomplishment came over me. It felt soft and warm. And I caught myself looking and feeling like that park ranger did on the first morning I arrived at the trail. I guess I understood why guys like Roger enjoyed the mountains like they did.

I decided to leave Jada and that town in Florida because nobody was talking about taking off and going on adventures. Everyone around me, including myself, was starting to slip away into that thirty or forty-year work routine, that *American Dream* routine, of non-stop work and credit card bills and mortgage payments and weekend trips twice a year. I wasn't ready for all that shit yet. All around Florida, I saw high school boys trading in their footballs and college dreams for a pack of Marlboros and a chance to be cool, and I didn't want to be a part of that *We Real Cool* crowd.

Jada never cared so much about following her own dreams or busting out at the seams with adventure—she talked about wanting a lover she could call her own and a job that allowed for weekend getaways to Savannah or Daytona. She loves driving her cute little sports car around town and shopping for new clothes every couple of months, but she doesn't care like I do about how our neighborhood is changing. Just give Jada a lover who doesn't take off on a six-month hiking trip, and she'll sleep soundly each night.

But I'll be honest, I was really starting to miss the way Jada looked at me in the mornings when she would get ready for work. I was missing those days when she got undressed again and crawled back into bed. We make great lovers, she and I, but we see things differently when it comes to adventure and the things we want for ourselves. She wants somebody to be her superhero, and I want to be able to look back on my life and say, "Wow, I'm really happy I did that."

But Jada loves me, and she tells me that all the time. And honestly, I need to hear that from her because I don't tell it to myself enough.

The temperature on top of Tray Mountain dropped quickly that night, and I was grateful to have already finished my dinner before Radar arrived at camp. He was visibly shaking in the cold as he changed his clothes and tried lighting his stove for cooking, and I just sat there watching him, already snug in my sleeping bag with a full belly. Watching him shiver in the cold like that made me feel warmer somehow, and I liked that. Snowflakes started showing up soon after that, and three other hikers scurried into camp after Radar did. I continued to smile as I watched all of them trying to get warm in the dark. All men were in the shelter that night, and I picked my toenails in my sleeping bag as they washed their dirty dishes and found a place to sleep on the shelter floor.

Leif and Radar and Speedy hung their food bags in nearby trees, and they told stories to each other about where they came from, where they went to school, and how they missed home-cooked meals. They seemed fond of each other, and I sat quietly listening. Chillkoot sat in the corner of the shelter with his headlamp on, scribbling the events of the day down in his journal. I sat listening to the laughter around me, and even though we were all strangers, it did feel like we were brothers in a way. We were brothers of the Appalachian Trail. I thought about the engraving I read on top of Springer Mountain, the one about "creating a fellowship with the wilderness," and it felt like I was watching that fellowship unfold a little bit before my eyes.

I thought about Rock and Little Rock, as I listened to those guys tell more of their stories.

I watched Chillkoot as he chewed on dry mango strips and wrote about things. I watched the pain on Leif's face as he unzipped his sleeping bag and removed his sock to show the rest of us how his big toe split right down the middle. It was a nasty gash. He dabbed the wound with a wet bandana as he picked the lint strands of wool from the bloody puss on his toe, but he breathed in deep and tried to play it cool, like he was a tough guy or something. He told us that it didn't hurt all that much, and I laughed to myself because *Leif ain't gonna let some bloody gash on his toe stop him from hiking on. No sir!* And I loved that look on his face during that moment, because that was the look of a superhero to me! *Damn.* I don't even know Leif, but he was a friggin' superhero that night because he powered through that split toe of his. He reminded me of the old San Diego Charger, Kellen Winslow, who, in that 1980s playoff football game against the Miami Dolphins achieved superhero status for me. Winslow went all out in that game, above and beyond, and I remember seeing that footage with my father, and how Winslow's teammates had to carry him off the field after his heroics helped them win that game in overtime. *And damn!* Leif was like Kellen Winslow to me that night. I respected the hell out of him as he wrapped a couple of napkins around his toe and tied it up with a piece of mole skin. *Damn!* Nothing was gonna stop him from getting to where he was going! Fucking superhero if you asked me. *Goddamn!*

It must've been around eight or nine o'clock at night when we heard someone else coming toward the shelter. We all sat up in our bags as we watched Mr. B trudge his way toward the camp with his headlight shining.

"Jesus Christ!" he said, as he dropped his pack on the shelter floor. "Could it get any friggin' colder out here?"

I slid my gear further up against the wall to give him space on the shelter floor, and the first thing he did when he sat down was to reach into his pocket for a smoke. I sat right up and said, "Hey, Mr. B, you got an extra one of those?"

"Hell yeah," he said. "Here, take the rest of the pack. I've got four more packs in my bag."

"Wow. Awfully nice of you, Mr. B," I said. "I appreciate it very much."

"Not to worry, my friend. Not to worry at all." He turned and looked me square in the face. "What's your name again?"

"Bird," I said. "My trail name is Bird. I met you at Neel's Gap."

"Well, it's good to see you again, Bird. It's always nice to share a smoke with someone for the first time."

I felt kinda shitty as I sat there smoking with Mr. B because I knew full well that I had nearly a carton of cigarettes still in my pack. But honestly, up to that point, I was embarrassed smoking in front of the other hikers, like it was forbidden or frowned upon or something. But once Mr. B did it, it opened the door for me to follow along, and I jumped at the chance. Maybe the other hikers would look at me as more of a part-time smoker, not full-time, like Mr. B. To them, maybe it looked like I smoked on occasion but not all the time. Maybe it looked like I could take it or leave it… and that's the way I wanted it to look. Little did they know I was a complete smoking fiend, and if I didn't have my nicotine fix fifteen or twenty times a day, then I'd be a complete wreck. I needed those smokes after every meal and several times in-between, but my favorite cigarette of the day, hands down, was the one right after I woke up. There's nothing like the syrupy, harsh taste of a Marlboro first thing in the morning!

Now that Mr. B led the way with smoking, I felt like I could smoke in front of everyone else every time he did. The others, however, started to snort and sniff and cough from their sleeping bags as Mr. B and I smoked at the edge of the shelter. Radar put out a fake cough a couple times, like one of my non-smoking ex-girlfriends used to do, but Mr. B just kept on smoking. So, I kept smoking right alongside him.

Mr. B was one of those hikers who had all the top-notch high-tech gear, and he used specialized ski poles as hiking sticks. "Two hundred bucks," he said, as he showed me the grips on the handles. "What else does a sixty-five-year-old have to spend his money on? Nothing! That's what." He talked about how he once attempted to hike the Appalachian Trail back in his thirties, but he had to pull off the trail after sixteen days when he fell and broke his ankle. "But now I'm back," he said, "and I have an unlimited budget all the way to Maine."

Chillkoot sat up in his bag, shook his head, and said, "Man, I'm trying to make it to Maine on twenty-eight hundred bucks!"

"Sucks being you," laughed Mr. B, "but good luck with that, kid."

It all seemed like fun and games for Mr. B, and he had a nonchalant, carefree approach to life on the trail. "Hey, let's have another smoke," he said, as he started to tell me about what he did for work. He worked as an engineer for Boeing, and now that he was retired, he was out to explore the world and finish the trail he started. "I gotta do it while I still have my legs under me. You know what I mean, Bird?"

Radar sat up from his bag and asked Mr. B about his family and whether he had kids and a wife. "Yeah, I got those things," said Mr. B, "but they have everything they need, and my wife kinda liked the idea of getting rid of me for six months." He laughed.

Radar started to say something about aviation and wanting to be a pilot, but Mr. B cut him off with, "Hey, any of you guys like college hoops? I like college hoops, so I'm gonna listen to the March Madness tournament on the radio. What about Duke? Any of you guys like Duke and Krzyzewski? They're playing the Orangemen tonight, and it's gonna be a great game. God, I love college hoops, but I hate Duke. No offense to any of you guys, but I hate those fuckin' Blue Devils. Let's go, Syracuse!" he said, as he put in his earphones to listen to the game.

Now, I like college hoops and all, but Mr. B must have assumed that everyone in the shelter that night liked college hoops too, and that everyone else wanted to be updated on the score every few minutes. "Duke by nine," said Mr. B a few minutes after putting in his earphones. Chillkoot chuckled from his corner spot in the shelter, as I put out my cigarette and zipped up my bag for the night. A few minutes later, "Duke by four." Leif rolled over in his bag with a sigh. A few minutes after that, "Tie Game!" Everyone in the shelter began to find the humor in Mr. B's commentary, and we sighed and laughed from our bags.

"Duke by five."

"Duke by eleven."

"Fuckin' Blue Devils," he mumbled a few minutes after that. "Duke won by nine."

Several inches of snow fell in the mountains that night, and my face was frosty as I sat up and tasted the cold morning air. I didn't sleep very well because Mr. B was mumbling nonsense all night in between grinding his teeth and snoring, like my mother used to do before the doctor gave her a plastic mouthguard to sleep with. Chillkoot was already mixing oatmeal and drinking coffee by the time I crawled out of my bag, and I didn't mind looking at the snow-covered hills and trees as my coffee warmed on the stove. The coffee felt warm and good in my hands, but then Radar pointed to my shirt hanging on the rafters and said, "Looks like it's frozen solid to me. It's gonna be brutal putting that thing on," he said. And he was right. The mistake I made of hanging my wet shirt up outside on a cold night in the mountains had me dreading the moment I had to put it back on. The shirt was stiff and crunchy when I tried to get into it, and if I'm honest, my balls shrank up and my nipples immediately got stiff when I put that thing over my chest. I couldn't breathe for a minute or so, and it took some time for the icy fabric to melt and turn warm with my body heat. "Jesus Christ!" I said, imitating Mr. B. "Could it get any friggin' colder right now!"

Chillkoot and Radar had smirks on their faces as they watched me struggle with my icy chill, and Leif said something about how nice a hot shower would be. Even my bootlaces were frozen as I tried to tie them. My feet felt trapped in blocks of ice as I limped my way behind the shelter to yellow the snow. Mr. B was still cozied up in his bag as the rest of us shouldered our packs and got ready for the day of hiking. There was no need for all of us to leave the shelter at the same time because we knew we'd more than likely see one another by the end of day, so one by one, the guys ventured off. Chilkoot and I were the last ones at camp other than Mr. B, and I wondered if Mr. B would make it as far as the rest of us that day. Even though we were all hiking the same trail, if Mr. B hiked less than we did for a few days, it wouldn't be long before we were miles and miles ahead of him. I thought about maybe never seeing him again, and I took an extra minute to look at Mr. B in his bag before I left with Chillkoot. *Duke by nine!* I thought. Hilarious.

Chillkoot was a big kid from the foothills of Vermont. He looked like a hockey player to me, bulky and strong with huge hands. He said he was hiking home to marry his high school sweetheart and raise a family. He said the thought of hiking back home to marry the love of his life kept him going on those tough stretches of uphill climbing and when it was raining like hell. He looked like a family man too, with his short brown hair parted on the side and his freshly shaved face. I found it interesting that he combed his hair each morning and took the time to shave. He looked mid-twenties with broad shoulders and trimmed fingernails—he looked like most young businessmen, just in hiking gear instead of a three-piece suit. Interesting. Chillkoot had long legs and a steady stride, and it wasn't long before he was a good distance ahead of me that morning.

And that was fine with me because it gave me a chance to have my morning smoke in private. Nothing is better than that morning smoke. Pretty soon, I couldn't see Chillkoot anymore because of how far ahead he was, and I was once again hiking with nothing but my Marlboros and my thoughts. I started laughing to myself with thoughts of Mr. B the night before. His 'Duke by nine' comments were funny as hell. He reminded me of my father when he said, "Jesus Christ!" about how cold it was.

My father shouted "Jesus Christ!" at me one time when I was nine or ten and playing basketball at the local youth center. He was coaching our team for one game as a 'fill-in' for our head coach, who was out of town, and my father paced up and down the court sidelines like a madman during that game. We were losing by a handful of points with only a minute or so left to go, and my father called a timeout to give us all that last-minute pep talk. My father gathered our team around and shouted "Jesus Christ!" at me because of how crappy I was playing. He grabbed a handful of my jersey with his fist and said, "What the hell's the matter with you, boy? You need to play better!" I could smell the alcohol on his breath, I could see the insane look in his eyes—my teammates started to back away from our little huddle because they feared they would be next. We ended up losing the game that day, and I remember the sad and defeated look on my father's face as we drove home.

I awoke from my daydream standing on top of Kelly Knob. Chillkoot was long gone by that point, and I realized I'd spent nearly half the day thinking about my father and youth basketball. Since morning, I had hiked deep down into Addis Gap before climbing all the way back up to the top of Kelly Knob. It took nearly four hours to travel that distance, but it only seemed like a moment, because I'd spent all that time thinking about my crazy-ass father and all the times I felt embarrassed and frightened because of him. If you had asked me where I had hiked that morning, I'd have no recollection. And I hated that! I hated how that man occupied so much of my mind, and I wrote about that in my journal. I hated having that bad taste of my father in my mouth. For a minute, I wished I was Chillkoot. The thought of hiking back to my sweetheart sounded pretty awesome compared to what I was hiking with. I mean, I was hiking away from Jada, not toward her, and I was hiking closer to the memories of the man I hated. I didn't know how to turn any of that off...

It was Christmas Eve, and I was eight years old. The whole family piled into the car, and father drove the quarter mile down the road to the local church. We considered ourselves half-ass Catholics back then because we only went to church two or three times a year, and Christmas Eve was one of those times. Us kids were still too young for the midnight mass, so we'd go to the nine o'clock service instead. Mother made sure our hair was combed and that we looked presentable with collared shirts and shoes, no sneakers. Father always drove, and on that Christmas Eve, he pulled into the church parking lot and told my mother that he wasn't going to the service. He said he'd wait for us in the car in the parking lot.

Mother paused and looked him up and down before saying, "Twice a year is too much to ask, huh?"

"Just go ahead," he said. "I'll be here when you get out."

Mother unbuckled her seatbelt, mumbled something under her breath, and then said, "Okay kids, let's go."

"Aren't you coming to church, dad?" asked my brother.

"No, not this time," he said. "But go ahead though, buddy. I'll be right here when you're done."

After the service, we found him sitting in the car in the back of the church parking lot with the engine running. Mother stood outside the driver's side door for a couple minutes with her arms folded across her chest. "Gimme the keys," she said. "I'll drive us home."

"What are you talking about, Christine. Get in the car," he said. "I'm driving."

Mother didn't budge, as she motioned for us kids not to get into the car.

"What are we waiting for?" said my sister. "Aren't we going home? I gotta pee."

"No," said my mother. "I think we'll walk home tonight kids. It's a beautiful night, so let's walk."

"What are you talking about?" said my brother. "It's freezing outside, and dad's right here. Why are we walking?"

"Yeah, and I gotta pee," said my sister.

Mother stepped back from the car door, turned back toward the church, looked up to the sky, and stood there for what seemed to be a long time.

"Come on, Christine! Just get in the car," said my father.

"Yeah," said my brother. "Come on, mom. Let's go."

Mother turned back to the car with a sigh and said, "Okay, kids. Let's go. Hop in, but be sure to buckle up."

"Thank, God!" said my sister. "I really gotta go."

Once inside the car, my mother started saying, "Can I please driv…."

"Christine!" interrupted my father. "Could you please shut up! Just shut up," he said. He pulled the car ahead to the exit of the church parking lot, and then he stopped the car. There weren't any cars coming from either direction, but my father sat there behind an idle engine at the exit of the church parking lot. He eventually looked at my mother and said, "Which way to the house?"

There was an anxious moment of silence as my mother turned to see if any of us kids heard what father said. "Left," said my brother. "Our house is to the left."

"Thanks, buddy," said my father, as he hit the gas and went left.

The next morning, we woke up to glasses of milk and cookies on the kitchen table. A bunch of presents were under the tree. "Where's dad?" asked my sister.

"He's still sleeping," said my mother. "Come on kids, let's open some presents without him."

Chillkoot was standing on the side of US Road 76 as I walked out of the woods. He had his thumb up in the air, and it wasn't a minute or two before a banged-up Chevy pickup pulled over and asked if we needed a ride to town.

"You coming?" asked Chillkoot.

"Hell yeah," I said, and we both jumped in back.

The town of Hiawassee, Georgia had a population of maybe a thousand people, and Chillkoot and I hopped out of the truck on the main strip at a big Hardees sign. We were both starving, so we feasted on burgers with cheese, crispy fries, fountain sodas, and warmed apple pies that came in a box. We rolled our eyes and laughed with each bite because it was the best shitty food we'd ever eaten. We felt like kings of the forest that day, feeding on two-dollar cheeseburgers and six-dollar meal deals. We both stocked up on packets of ketchup and mustard and salt and pepper from the condiment rack. Chillkoot stuffed a handful of napkins into his pocket, and I was quick to do the same. "I'm tired of wiping my ass with leaves," he said, laughing.

"I hear that," I said. "Those smooth stones are really cold!" We both laughed.

With mud and dirt up to our knees and all over our clothes, we were certain that we smelled pretty ripe to the other customers in the restaurant. But they didn't seem to mind, and many of them came up to us and asked us if we were thru-hikers on our way to Maine. One little kid poked his mother in the side as they stood in line, saying, "Look, mom. They're hikers!"

Strangers walked by and wished us luck, and just like with our trip into town, it only took a minute or two for us to find another free ride back to the trail head. With full bellies, Chillkoot and I stretched our legs and pushed forward. We were laughing and smiling because we knew that North Carolina was only a few miles ahead.

6:46pm

Our mother would come home from work each day and the first thing she'd do was turn down the heat. "How many times do I have to tell you guys that seventy degrees is warm enough!"

My sister hated wearing sweaters and thick socks around the house in the winter. Mother pinched pennies wherever she could, and none of us kids got fat on the food stamps. "When are you going shopping again, mom? There ain't nothing to eat around here."

"There isn't anything to eat," she'd say, correcting us.

My brother got an after-school job because he got tired of the Goodwill store hand-me-downs that mother could afford, and I remember when Andy took that job with Roger after he graduated high school. He loved that job, and when I asked him why he left it, he said it was because Roger was too old, and he needed to go into a nursing home.

6

A short-lived hoot-and-holler type celebration took place midway up the face of Sharp Top Mountain because nailed to the side of a massive oak tree was a sign announcing our last step in Georgia and our first step in North Carolina. Chillkoot shook my hand and said, "One state down and only twelve more to go."

"Nothing to it," I said, shrugging my shoulders. We both laughed. I thought it was pretty cool to put one foot in Georgia and the other in North Carolina—like I was splitting myself in two—one foot in yesterday and one foot in tomorrow sort of thing. I looked forward to hiking in North Carolina and leaving Georgia behind.

Every thru-hiker had issues they were dealing with other than the trail they hiked. Externally, there was the rocky terrain, the up and down climbing, the blisters, the rain, the weight of things carried; but internally, we dealt with things like hunger and thirst, fear, and loneliness. I read a book in high school by Tim O'Brien called *The Things They Carried,* and I'd be a liar if I said I didn't feel a little like that guy did. I liked reading that book because it was raw and frightening and heavy and real. O'Brien wrote a lot about being in the Vietnam War, but he also wrote about the

86

people surrounding him and how those people helped him get through a lot of the tough internal stuff. No, I wasn't fighting in Vietnam or Afghanistan or Russia or anything like that, but I sure as hell had a war going on inside of me.

At one point in O'Brien's book, he wrote about being in a boat on a river; Canada was on one side of the river and the United States was on the other side. He wanted to escape the draft by jumping off that boat and swimming over to Canada, but there was something holding him back and he didn't do it. And even though I wasn't on the Canadian border in a boat, or anything like that, I could feel this tug of war inside my chest. When I had one foot in Georgia and the other in Carolina, it was like I was stepping out of yesterday and into tomorrow, and part of me didn't want to go there. I didn't want my tomorrow to be anything like my father's.

Radar and Leif caught up with Chillkoot and me at Muskrat Creek Shelter. It was late in the afternoon, and Radar dropped his pack on the shelter floor with a heavy sigh. He was happy to be done for the day, and he was excited to cook up some rice and Spam for dinner. Leif was also done for the day, and he wasted no time in hanging his wet things on a clothesline. But Chillkoot strapped himself back into his pack and said he still had five miles left to go because he wanted to get to Standing Indian Shelter. With a tip of his imaginary cap, Chillkoot said, "So long," and was off.

I liked Radar and Leif just fine, but Chillkoot was the only other hiker who traveled at the same pace I did. Up to that point, I was the only one passing other hikers. I would pass them at some point in the day, and maybe they would end up spending the night in the same place as me, but other hikers weren't passing me throughout the day; it was the other way around. I had a feeling that I wouldn't see Mr. B again, and I had a similar feeling about Radar and Leif—it was only a matter of a day or two before I put enough distance between myself and them. But Chillkoot was different. He passed me every day, and I was trying to keep up with him. He was the one who might lose me instead of me losing him. So, like Chillkoot before me, I shouldered my pack again, tipped my cap to Leif and Radar, and I was off for Standing Indian Shelter.

"Have a good hike," said Radar.

"See you down the trail," said Leif.

We'll see about that, I thought.

The shelter at Standing Indian Mountain was just south of the mountain itself. I dropped my pack on the shelter floor and said hello to Chillkoot. The sun hadn't set yet, and I stood in amazement at the size of the mountain in front of me. I'd never seen a chunk of earth that big before, and I didn't like the thought of having to climb that Standing Indian first thing in the morning. "That's gonna be a hell of a climb first thing," I said.

"I'd rather get it out of the way early," said Chillkoot. "After that, the day doesn't seem too tough," he said. "I got nineteen miles planned for tomorrow. How about you?"

"Yeah, I don't know about tomorrow," I said, still staring at that mountain. "It sure is a pain in the ass way to start the morning though." I opted not to tell him I only had twelve miles planned for the next day.

It was only me and Chillkoot in the shelter that night, and he decided to pitch his tent on a grassy patch beside the shelter. "Those shelter floors are pretty tough on my back," he said, "and this patch of grass here looks like a pretty nice cushion to me."

"Smart," I said.

He went to bed just as the sun went down, and I liked the thought of eating granola and smoking cigarettes by myself in the shelter. I couldn't get the thought of hiking up Standing Indian first thing in the morning out of my head. That mountain was the only thing I could see in front of me, so I smoked and ate cheese as I stared at that mountain. I rubbed my feet and replaced the moleskin on my heels. I smoked more.

I wasn't up for sleeping because of too much thinking, so I pulled out my journal and started writing. I wrote about Rock and Little Rock. I wrote about the blackbird that circled high above Springer Mountain before diving down into the treetops. I wrote about his empty claws. I wrote about Mr. B and the 'fellowship' that I was supposed to create with the wilderness. "Duke by nine," I wrote. I wrote about belt-buckle Bob and the tobacco-chewing kid at Tritt's. I could still see the brown tobacco stains on the corners of his mouth. I even wrote about my mother and the decision she made to divorce our father.

The earth around me fell fast asleep as the darkness settled in, and I wrote about Jada and the warmth of our Florida apartment. I wrote about never wanting to take things for granted again, like running water and a toilet that flushed. I wrote about my brother and sister, and I tried not to write about my father. I smoked another cigarette as I wrote more about my mother. I wondered what that guy, Tim O'Brien, felt like as he fell asleep in the jungles of

Vietnam. I wondered what his story would be like these days if he decided to swim over to Canada that day on the boat? My feelings were scattered as I thought about my childhood and the times when our family was still a family.

By seven the next morning, I felt like the old car that had been sitting in the garage too long. My body ached in strange places, and I stretched my neck and legs to loosen up. My boots felt clumsy, and my arms felt weak. I remembered how my mother used to go out early on those winter mornings to start up her Volkswagen hatchback some fifteen minutes before she'd leave for the day, and I felt like that car, loud muffler and all. I needed coffee. I needed a smoke. I waited for Chillkoot to leave before I fired up.

Standing Indian Mountain was so big that it took up half the sky. Now that it was daylight and the sun was rising, I could see every nook and cranny of that rock, and I was intimidated by it. I thought about spending the day in my sleeping bag. That mountain was a 5,500-foot climb straight up, and I couldn't understand how Chillkoot left camp that morning with a smile on his face and a pep in his step. I had met my match with Chillkoot, and I knew it. I was not looking forward to that climb, and I knew my toughest step would be the first, so I shouldered my pack and went to it.

By eight o'clock, my breath was gone. By nine o'clock, I was soaked in sweat. By ten, the straight uphill climb leveled off a bit, and I stopped and smoked. The summit was getting close, but the steep stretch of trail near the top of Standing Indian forced me to crawl along at a snail's pace. The trail itself might have been twelve inches wide in parts, and to my immediate right there was a drop-off of at least a thousand feet on to the tops of tall pine trees. I've never been all that fond of heights, and that drop-off forced me to look the other way. *Jesus Christ!* To my left was a huge slab of stone that went straight up, and I had to walk sideways through that stretch of trail, hugging the rock face as I shuffled along. One false move, and I would have been lost forever in those pine trees below. *Don't look down. Don't look down.*

I could hear voices as I approached the summit of Standing Indian. Three college guys from Georgia Tech were taking some time away from their studies by hiking, drinking tequila from the bottle, and roasting hot dogs over an open flame. They sat on tree stumps around a fire pit, and they laughed about this and that as they welcomed me. I dropped my pack on the ground next to them and fired up a smoke. It was hardly noon, but they were well on their way to polishing off that bottle of tequila. They passed it my way, and I declined. They offered me a hot dog on a stick, and I accepted.

"You hiking to Maine?" asked one of them.

"That's the plan," I said.

I took a seat around their fire, and they told me about the other hiker, Chillkoot, that passed through about an hour earlier. They offered me another hot dog and asked me several questions about trail life. I wasn't up for much chit-chat with those guys because I knew if I stopped for too long, I'd get cold and stiff and wouldn't be up for more hiking. Those guys seemed nice enough, but I didn't want to spend my day by the fire watching them fall off their tree stumps. I took their hot dogs with a smile, strapped my pack back on, and wished them well.

"Good luck with your hike," said one of them, with a fist in the air and a near fall from his stump.

The smell of burning pine and the sounds of their laughter faded as I descended from the summit, and I smoked my smoke in silence and thought about those Georgia Tech guys. I never went to college, and I often wondered what life on campus would be like for a guy like me. I wanted to be a scientist as a kid, but that was only a phase—I reached the point of trading in my imaginary lab coat for my own bottle of tequila with likeminded friends. I knew that drinking and drugging every day wasn't a good fit for me, and that's why I stopped when I did, but I was envious of those Georgia Tech guys doing the college thing. I thought about my life as an uneducated sober guy, and then I compared it to the life of a drunk college kid with a degree. I wondered who would have the easier life moving forward? I liked the fact that I wasn't drinking anymore, but I thought about how hard life would be without that college degree. I smoked and I hiked as I thought about education and tequila.

Big Spring Shelter came into sight as did the faces of several other hikers I hadn't met yet. Strawberry was tending to a fire in the pit, and Saluki was sitting on the edge of the shelter floor, eating granola from a plastic bag. Fargo was also new to me, and she hung her clothes on a line that went over Strawberry's fire. Chillkoot was there too, and he was mixing noodles in a pot on his stove. I said hello to all of them, and they all smiled back. But then I smelled that all-too-familiar smell of weed, and man, I used to love smoking weed! It only took one whiff to make me miss it all over again. I looked around for the source of the smell, and when I looked deep into the back corner of the shelter, I could see the orange glow of the joint being smoked. I could see the shadow of some dark figure, and as I walked over to say hello, his face came into sight more. I didn't get his name, but he sat cross-legged in army pants. He was very quiet and bald, tugging on his joint, and his stern face and knee-high boots implied that he wasn't up for much talking. I said hello anyway as I set up my stove for cooking, and he nodded slowly and smoked more.

I ate my white rice and beans and made more coffee as I watched the other hikers around the camp. They all had different routines with cooking and cleaning, and the chatter around the fire was easygoing and cheerful. The fire roared, and Strawberry's face glowed as she sat close to the ring and warmed her hands. She was with Fargo, and the two of them were from Nevada—best friends since they were kids, and now that they had both finished college at the University of California, they were hiking the trail before getting jobs and settling down someplace. Saluki was from Illinois, and he too was recently out of school. He talked about maybe going back to get his doctorate, but he was taking time for himself in between.

They all had a plan, and I'd be a liar if I said I wasn't jealous of their plans. All that talk of college and doctorates and settling down in a career—it made me feel less than everyone around me—everyone except that quiet army guy in the corner, who still wasn't talking to anyone. Everyone else simply ignored him, but I felt like I had more in common with him than the others. I'd never been in the military, but I knew what it was like to stay quiet in a cloud of smoke for days on end. I knew what it felt like to sit on the outskirts of everything that was going on.

After my coffee was finished brewing, I happily stirred in the Hardee's sugar packets and powdered cream I swiped. The coffee felt warm in my hands, and it didn't take long for me to decide that I didn't want to spend the night there. I wasn't interested in sharing space with the quiet guy in the corner, so I laced my boots back up and asked Chillkoot if he was up for a night hike.

"I'm done for the day, Bird, but I'll take a raincheck on the night hike. Night hikes are great."

I was yet to hike at night, but it was only five more miles to the next shelter, so I strapped on my headlamp and nodded to those I'd just met. I felt better about getting away from that bald army guy in the corner.

The woods at night seemed quieter. Every noise seemed that much louder. The wind stirred more at night, and every snapped twig caused me to stop and look around. My heartbeat was faster hiking at night. My muscles were more sore hiking at night. The trail was bumpier at night, and my pack felt heavier. My first impression of night hiking wasn't a good one—everything was ominous and shaded black.

My brother had this crazy theory when we were kids growing up. He used to say that if you were ever freezing cold while you were waiting for the school bus to come, then you should close your eyes and think about someplace warm. "It really works," he used to say. "Just think of someplace warm, like a sunny beach in Florida, and you won't be cold anymore."

I used to tell him that his theory was bullshit, but he still believed it, and he would use that theory with just about anything. Like, when he'd ask a girl to be his girlfriend and she'd say no, he just turned it all around in his head as if he was the one saying no. Or, if our father came home all drunk and violent, he would just close his eyes and pretend dad was sober and happy.

I used to tell him to grow up. "If dad's drunk," I'd say, "then he's fucking drunk. And if the girl says no, then she says no. If you're cold, then you're fucking cold, and there ain't no amount of pretending that will ever change those things. It is what it is," I used to tell him.

And it's all pretty funny now, when I look back on it, because I'd be a liar if I said I wasn't using my brother's theory that night when I was hiking. I mean, I never closed my eyes or anything, but I did think about it being daytime instead of nighttime. I did think about my life as being just as relevant as those other hikers who were taking breaks from getting their doctorates and all. I did think of myself as a good guy and not some loser sitting quietly in the dark corners getting high. And it's all really funny too, because I was definitely trying to use my brother's theory that night in those dark woods. It was dark, and I was scared. It was dark, and I pretended it was light outside. It was friggin' cold, and I started pretending I was warm in sunny Florida, just like my brother used to do.

The surface-bound roots, the bumpy rocks, and the slick moss along the trail, always had me looking down. The moment I tried to look up to see what was going on around me would be the moment I slipped or tripped or twisted an ankle or a knee. Instinctively, I wanted to look up, so I had to force myself to always look down. If I wanted to look up, I had to stop hiking, or else. If I stopped though, then I wouldn't be moving forward, and that was the problem. Naturally, I would test this by looking up briefly, but I gotta say, once I fell the first time, twisting my ankle, I accepted the fact that I always had to be looking down. And I hated the trail sometimes because of this. I wanted to see the beauty of those woods as I walked through them, and I hated the fact that I couldn't. I continuously felt like I was missing something. I hated some of the elements I had to endure too, like the freezing rain and blisters on my heels, but I was somehow starting to feel grateful for being out there in those elements. Weird.

Emotionally, I struggled, because internally, I was being pushed and pulled in all sorts of different directions. I started thinking about my sister and all the times I told her I hated her when we were kids. She was such a pain in the ass back then, but the truth was, I loved her. Always have. I thought about our father and how I never wanted to be like him. But then I thought about how I never really knew him. He was a private man, and I hated that my mother told me I was a lot like him. I thought about my mother too, and how I never really let her in. I always kept her an arm's length away. And all those thoughts led to actual tugs in my gut, for real, and those tugs had me wishing that things were different. I imagined telling my sister that I loved her instead of hating her. I imagined accepting my father for who he was, and for the things he did to us. I thought about hugging my mother again. I thought about my brother and all the stupid shit we used to do together…

We gave ourselves sixty seconds to get the job done. We had one minute to get as much as we could. The five of us stood across the street, and we waited for the last car to pull away from the convenience store. It was nearly dark, and the five of us boys had spent the day drinking around my mother's kitchen table. I can't remember whose idea it was, maybe Paul's, but one of us suggested robbing the convenience store down the street. We all sat around in silence for a minute or so, waiting for the one coward to say, "Hell, no. I ain't doing it." But nobody said that, and a few minutes later, I was digging through the winter clothes in my closet looking for ski hats and gloves. I found some old clothes, and we all put them on, all five of us. I pulled a switchblade from my desk drawer, and we cut eye holes in our hats to make masks. When we were all ready, we walked the back streets and cut through yards to get to the store. We gave ourselves sixty seconds.

We went over the plan several times as we waited for that last car to pull away. And when that time finally came, we dropped our hats over our faces and walked toward the door. "Don't fuck this up," said Paul.

I took a deep breath and swung the door open. I pulled the knife from my pocket and immediately went toward the girl behind the counter. Paul stayed outside the door to be the lookout. Two of the others, Greg and Rob, went after all the cigarettes they could jam into their pockets. My brother stayed beside me as a backup. The girl behind the counter was younger than I was, and I recognized her from school. I remembered the time I said hello to her at the summer carnival, but she and I were never friends or anything like that. This time was obviously different, and she looked deep into the eye holes of my mask as I raised the knife to her neck.

"Forty-five seconds," said my brother.

Greg and Rob laughed as they fumbled with the cartons of cigarettes they were trying to stuff into their coats.

I looked that girl square in the face, knife to her throat, and I told her to open the cash drawer. She was shaking, and I could see the tears form in her eyes. I told her to stay calm and open the drawer. Once the drawer was open, she pulled out all the cash and placed it in my hands.

"Thirty seconds," said my brother.

After I had all the money, I told her to walk to the back of the store. She was crying now, but to her credit, she did exactly as I said. Once there, I told her to close her eyes and slowly count to one hundred. "After that," I said, "feel free to call the cops."

The five of us ran back through the yards and side streets as fast as we could until we reached the train tracks outside our neighborhood. We ripped off our masks and took a minute or two to catch our breath. We looked around at one another, and nobody needed to say anything. We knew we wouldn't talk about it to anyone. We heard the police sirens in the distance as we split the money, cigarettes, and candy. It was a pretty good score, and we knew it. We burned our ski masks beside the tracks before going home.

I never said a word to anyone about that robbery, and neither did my brother. The local cops had their suspicions about us, but nothing ever came of it. Apparently, the girl behind the counter said it was someone in their thirties or forties, so the cops didn't pay much attention to us teenagers. I remember how strange it was when that same girl smiled and said hello to me in the school corridor the next time I saw her. All I could do was smile back and say hello…

I'm not sure why the dark hillsides and mountains of the Appalachian Trial stirred my memories and brought about my confessions, but they did. Those darker truths about my past had been locked away in my chest for years, and I'd done all that I could to keep those memories bottled up and hidden. I threw the keys to those memories away years ago, and I preferred it that way, so I wondered about those mountains, and why they caused me to confess my sins and tell the truth.

I'm not sure how those peaks and valleys and all that hiking and sweating were able to melt away my tough outer shell, but it happened, and the truth of my past was now present, on the surface, hard to taste, and even harder to swallow. My chest felt like an open wound, and as I looked around for a witness to all my confessions, all I could see was myself. Who else would be there in those woods to hear about my sins? Who else would be there to pass judgment on me and sentence me? Who else would be there to look down on me and walk away from me? The more I looked around, the only one I saw was me. And the more I saw of me, the less I saw of everything else. I wanted someone else there in those woods to hear my confessions, because then, I would have the distraction I was looking for. If anyone else was there, then I wouldn't have to look only at myself. *Fuck it*. I lit a cigarette and hiked on.

The next day, I could hear the distant hum of cars up ahead, and I knew a shelter was close by. Rock Gap Shelter was located just south of Old US 64, and it was a relief to drop my pack on those hardwood floors. I skipped cooking a meal that night because my hunger had been eaten away by Marlboros and thinking about my past. I smoked cigarettes and rubbed my temples as the sun began to set. I was alone in the shelter again, and the cars on Old 64 had me thinking about hitching a ride into town come morning. I would go to town and eat eggs and bacon and toast. I would go to town, and I would eat all those shitty memories back down to where they came from. I fell asleep that night with thoughts of what else I'd eat in the morning once I got to town...

"What's that you're writing?" asked an old-time Carolina man sitting across from me in some Franklin, North Carolina breakfast place.

"It's a journal," I said.

"Ahh, I see. You a writer?" he asked.

"Sorta."

"I've been published a couple of times myself," he said. "Small stuff mostly. I did a real nice piece about UFOs and the aliens living in my bedroom closet, and in my cellar and all. People really liked that one," he said.

Oh Jesus, I thought.

"It was one helluva story," he said. "Fiction, of course, cuz I ain't never really seen a UFO before… well, unless I count that time at Burgess Field around midnight when all of a sudden…."

That old-timer just went on and on with his story about some UFO that landed in some Carolina field, and how aliens now lived in his bedroom closet and so on. Out of respect, I pretended to listen, and I kept eye contact with him as I ate. I didn't register much of what he was saying because I was fascinated with how thin he was, and how his body moved around as he told his story. He talked with his hands like he was from New Jersey, but he moved his body like he was auditioning for some elderly dance competition. He had caved-in cheeks and pale, whitish lips that stretched wide in order to hold the dentures in his mouth. His thinning gray hairline gave way to visible eczema splotches and irritated patches all over his scalp, and dandruff continuously fell onto the shoulders of his checkered flannel shirt as he spoke. Every now and again, he swept away the flakes from his shirt onto the floor. His back was slightly hunched forward, and he wore dark-tinted glasses that made him look like one of the aliens he talked about living in his closet.

I had him pegged for a widower because of the ring he still wore, and the fact that he was in a booth set up for two. He had a place setting at the table with a napkin and silverware for someone who never came. I started feeling bad for that old-timer as he went on and on, but there was no indication he felt sorry for himself. He spoke very fast, as if his speech had trouble keeping up with the story in his head, and every now and again he'd reach over and touch a book he had with him. Strange. He couldn't seem to go longer than thirty seconds without reaching over and touching that book. He touched all the condiments on the table too. In between his thoughts, he would reach over to make sure the salt and pepper shakers were exactly where he wanted them. He used cream in his coffee, and each plastic creamer had to be stacked inside the others after he used them. He had six empty creamers in his stack as we talked. My guess was that he had a system for everything, and those were probably the ticks and habits and routines that helped distract him from thinking about his lost wife.

I couldn't help myself any longer. I'm not sure why I did it, but I did. "What's that you're reading?" I asked.

His back got stiff, and he rubbed his hands together with excitement. "I'm reading this here book about Area 51," he said, as he picked it up and showed me the cover. "It's a great book," he said, "and I know, without a shadow of a doubt, that the government is keeping aliens in that place. Personally, I think that some of the aliens have escaped, and that's why I've got one of them living in my closet at the house."

A part of me wished I kept my mouth shut, but it was too late at that point. I figured it would take me another five or so minutes to finish my meal, and then I'd be on my way, so I didn't see the harm in keeping things going.

The old man looked around the dining room of the restaurant before he asked if he could join me at my table. I didn't have the heart to say no, so he made his way over to my table. "So, you're a writer?" he asked.

I paused on purpose. I looked around. "I'm a journalist actually."

"Really!" he said.

"Yeah, I work for National Geographic," I said, "and they have me out here on assignment because they want me to take land samples along this section of the Appalachian Trail."

The old man was hooked at that point as he leaned in over the table with excitement. "What type of samples do they want? What are they looking for?" he asked.

It was hard for me to keep a straight face and stay focused because the splotches of flaking scalp skin on his head were so close to my food. I looked around the dining room again to make sure nobody was around or listening. "I'm testing the soil in these here woods because my company thinks there's something going on in this range of mountains."

"Like what?" he said. "What sort of something are you talking about?"

I leaned in a little closer, and with a soft whisper, I said, "Now this is top secret stuff here, so you can't say nothing to nobody."

"Absolutely," he said. "Mum's the word with me."

"Well, my company believes that there's some type of alien life form living here in these woods because of how remote they are, and they want me to test the soil for any foreign substances. You know what I mean?"

"I knew it!" he shouted, with the excitement of a little kid.

"Shhh, shhh!" I said. "Not so loud."

"Okay, okay," he said. "Sorry."

"I'm serious though. My company really thinks this is true, and I gotta tell ya, I've found some really interesting samples out there."

"Noooo."

"Yeah. And it's strange, too," I said. "I couldn't believe it when you started telling me your UFO story because that's exactly why I'm here. The fact is, I thought you might have been tracking me or something."

"Tracking you?"

"Yeah. I thought you might be here with a different outfit, a government agency or something, and you were following me around to keep tabs on what I was doing."

"Ohhh, I gotcha," he said. "Naw, that ain't me. I ain't following ya."

"Well, that's a relief," I said. "You had me worried there for a minute."

"My God!" he said in a whisper. "I just knew there was something going on around here. I just knew it. After my wife passed a couple of years back, I started hearing all these noises, and seeing things around the house that just weren't there before."

"Yeah," I said. "Aliens for sure."

"No shit," he said.

"No shit. But you gotta keep this between us," I said. "I've got sworn secrecy with this mission I'm on, and I'll lose my job if they find out I've been talking to you about this."

"Mum's the word, my friend. Mum's the word."

"Okay, good."

"I just can't believe that National Geographic would be in on this sorta thing," he said.

"Oh yeah," I said. "They have their hands in all sorts of different things. But this issue here is the one they're really counting on. Once they have proof of alien life in these here woods, it'll be front-page news for everyone to see. Front-page."

"Wow. Right here in these woods?"

"Yep, right here in these woods. But listen, I gotta get going. I gotta get back to those mountains and my testing."

"Oh, right, right," he said.

"But it was nice meeting you and chatting with you about this. Remember, Mum's the word, right?"

"Mum's the word," he said, covering his mouth.

I just couldn't believe how much I had that old boy eating on every one of my words! It wasn't so much a case of me trying to convince him of anything new; it was more a case of me feeding him more of what he already believed to be true. That old man was in his glory as we talked, and he waved goodbye to me like some madman as I strapped myself back into my pack and left that breakfast place. I could've felt worse than I did, I suppose, about stringing him along like that, but I didn't. I figured it would give him something to think about for the rest of the day. And truth be told, it gave me something to think about too. It was great fun meeting that old guy.

It was midmorning in Franklin, North Carolina, and I decided to walk back to the trailhead rather than hitch a ride. All around me, I saw cars buzzing here and there and mothers pushing babies in carriages through the parking lot of the local grocery store. I saw the red and white candy cane stripe of the local barber shop and little boys dressed in their Little League uniforms, glove in hand. I saw the old-school payphone out in front of the local fire station, and I decided to stop and make a call.

The phone rang a few times before she answered. "Good afternoon. Financing department. Can I help you?"

And there she was! There was the voice of the girl I missed so much. There was that colorful and smooth voice that I dreamed about the night before, and... "Ah, yes, miss," I said, with some disguise in my voice. "I've been on the line here for over an hour, and I've been back and forth with several different representatives from your company, and I'm getting a little frustrated with the fact that I can't seem to get any help with my financing issues, and I'm sorry, but I'm getting a little sick and tired of being pushed from one phone person to the next, and can you please put someone on the line that can help me with my issues because...."

"Well, sir," she interrupted. "I'm sorry for any inconvenience, but if you want, I can...."

"If I want!" I shot back. "What I *want* is someone who can help me! What I *want* is an accurate quote! What I *want* is someone who knows what the hell they're talking about, rather than dishing me off to the next department! *That's* what I want!"

"Sir. I'm sure I can work all of this out for you, but I'm going to ask you to calm down and tell me exactly what it is I can help you with."

Oh, she took a big chance by telling me I needed to calm down, but she was so strong and sweet and even-tempered with her delivery—how could I stay angry at that? I decided to dial down my response. "I'm sorry, miss, but did you just tell me I needed to calm down after I've been waiting on hold for over an hour? Is that what you're telling me?"

"Yes sir, that's exactly what I'm telling you. Now, I'm willing to do whatever I can to help you with your issues, so bear with me for a minute, and please tell me your account number."

Wow, she really did do a masterful job with that! "Yes, miss, you're exactly right, and I'd like to apologize for overreacting, and for the tone of my voice."

"That's no problem, sir. Can I please have your account number?"

I decided it was time to remove my disguise. "What I really wanted to tell you is that I miss you."

There was a pause in the line. "Excuse me," she said. "Who's this?"

"That was an excellent job you did," I said, "biting your tongue like that."

"Baby, is that you?"

"Haha. How you doing, sweet girl?"

"Ya know, I'm gonna beat your ass the next time I see you! They monitor these calls, ya know."

"Oh, but you did such a great job with your sweet, understanding voice."

"You're such an asshole!"

"Yeah, yeah. I know."

We talked and laughed for nearly an hour while she was still on the clock, and she told me about how cold our bed was at night and how she hadn't slept naked since I left. She told me about the flu bug she'd been fighting and how everybody at work was under the weather. "And I saw Robert the other day," she added.

"Oh yeah," I said. "How is Robert these days?"

"Baby, he asked me to borrow twenty bucks. He said it was for gas, and I ended up giving it to him, but I wasn't sure if I should've."

"For gas?" I said. "Yeah, that's not a good sign. With the amount he's been working, there shouldn't be any reason for borrowing money like that from a friend."

"I know, I know," she said. "But I didn't know what else to do when he asked me?"

"It's okay, baby. You did the right thing. But now that you've given him money once, there's a good chance he'll be back around asking for more."

"Oh Jesus!" she said. "I didn't even think of that. What should I say if he does?"

"Tell him you don't have it. Tell him… Tell him you just sent all your money to me because I needed extra cash on the trail."

"Oh, that's a good idea," she said. "I'll say that if he asks again."

I promised to write her a letter and to call her again when I could. It was tough to hang up with her; I didn't want to. She was at work, so she had to go anyway, but it was hard for me to say goodbye. Sure, I was having some fun with UFOs and the old-time boy I met that morning, but I knew the rest of the day had me walking alone. The rest of the day was me with me. No distractions.

I carried on with my heavy pack and new thoughts of Robert. Borrowing twenty bucks from a friend like that is never a good sign for a drug addict. I should have called him while I was in Franklin, but I didn't. I should have checked in on him, but I didn't. Once I got back to the trail, I kept my head down as I hiked. I couldn't afford to trip or fall on any of the roots or small stones beneath me.

7:52pm

Andy and I used to play football together in the street in front of our house when we were younger. He was the bigger and stronger one, so he would always be the quarterback. He would tell me to run as fast as I could to the Buick parked in front of the Delaney's house, then turn around and look for the ball.

I wasn't as talented as my brother at football, and I dropped more passes than I caught, but there were other things I was good at. My brother was the better athlete, but I was the better prankster. I used to love playing tricks on people and pushing their buttons. I like to think that Andy got his prankster skills from me.

It's interesting that Andy didn't remember that it was me who suggested we rob the store that day, but it was. I never thought we'd go through with it like we did, and just like my brother said, I never mentioned it to anybody after it happened.

7

I stood at the edge of the Nantahala River, and I watched the flow of the current as it curled its way around the base of Swim Bald Mountain. The river current was swift and strong, and I watched as a couple of kayakers passed me by. They wore orange life jackets and neon green helmets, and they laughed and smiled as they steered their way around boulders in the water and small drop-offs in the river. They waved as they passed me by, and I waved back.

I could feel myself adjusting to the way of life on the trail. It wasn't so much the physical adjustment of hiking ten to fifteen miles a day, it was more the emotional adjustment of spending so much time by myself. I could feel my newly formed calf muscles and how they burned during the day and then tighten up at night when I tried to fall asleep. If I didn't stretch my legs several times during the day, they would cramp and throb at night. I would lie on the ground sometimes during the day and elevate my legs against a tree to keep the blood flow circulating. The twenty or so extra pounds I carried around my waist for years quickly disappeared on the trail, and I could feel how my face was thinning out when I touched it. The once boyish round features of my cheeks were now chiseled with pronounced cheekbones and a defined chin that felt more like an elbow. In pools of water, I could see that my eyes were still the same, but my hair was getting long, wavy, and wild. I drank more water than ever before, but my thirst never seemed to be quenched. I ate more food than ever before, but I never felt full.

I felt good about the physical changes I could see on the outside—I mean, who doesn't want to lose some fat and gain some muscle? Physically, I was feeling lighter and stronger, and I liked that. But I could feel my emotions banging around on my insides, and I was becoming more aware that I no longer had access to my daily distractions that would allow me to avoid looking closely at them. I mean, in the real world, I worked forty to fifty hours a week, and I spent all that time thinking about the job at hand, the money I would make, and the boss I was trying to please. In the real world, I had Jada by my side, cars to drive, and TVs to watch. I had computers to search, friends to call, and refrigerators full of food. In the real world, I had running water at the twist of a wrist and a thermostat to adjust when things got too hot or too cold. The real world was full of distractions, but now those distractions were gone, and I was becoming increasingly aware. The emotions that were always easy to avoid, now seemed awake and unavoidable.

My father was a big football fan, and he made sure my brother and I knew everything about that game. He brought us to our first game when we were only kids, and he would talk to us about the Patriots and Giants and the men who played that game. He loved the physicality of that sport and the blood and sweat those men would shed. He taught us the rules of football, and he would quiz us on those rules when we least expected it. We'd be in line at the supermarket, and he'd say, "What does offsides mean?" We'd be driving someplace in the car, and he'd randomly say, "What does a linebacker do?" We'd be fishing down at the pond, and he'd say, "Who's the most important player on the football field?" He would quiz us at the dinner table and when we were brushing our teeth. He would quiz us at the playground and when we were doing our homework. He loved football.

For some people, Sunday would be the day for family visits and resting and nice clothes at church. For some people, Sunday would be the day for taking long drives and visiting friends, but that was not what Sunday was about in our house when we were kids. Sunday at our house was about football and beer. My father would spend every Sunday afternoon in his recliner chair with a beer in one hand and his yardstick in the other. My brother and I were forced to sit with him when the games were on, and he would use his yardstick to point at different players and different situations on the TV screen. "Do you see how he did that?" he'd say, pointing at the player with his stick. "Okay. It's third and eight," he'd say. "What should they do here to get the first down?"

"They should throw the ball," we'd say.

"Good," he'd say. "Who should they throw the ball to?"

"They should throw it to the fast guy on the outside."

"No, no," he'd say. "They should throw a screen pass to the running back over the middle because the defense is being too aggressive."

Then the play would happen, and the quarterback would try to throw the ball downfield to the fast guy running on the outside. It would fall incomplete, and my father would say, "See! See that! They should have thrown it to the running back over the middle. He was wide open!" My brother and I would just agree with him.

My rhythm for the trail had slipped away, and I struggled with the uphill climb on Swim Bald Mountain. That section of trail was full of switchbacks and zigzags, and even though I was getting closer to the summit, I was grunting and sweating and swearing and throbbing. I didn't feel like one of the football players my father used to speak of on Sundays because my body was sizzling, and my lungs were burning. I often thought of how I wanted to stop hiking, just give in and quit.

After climbing Swim Bald, however, I could see the Nantahala River a couple thousand feet below, and it looked like a stream of urine flowing down a dirt path. It was hard to believe that only a few hours earlier, I was standing by that river's edge. The groups of kayakers along the river now looked like colorful ants that got caught up in the current. I couldn't believe I had climbed so high without stopping. I was near the summit, so I kept on hiking, sizzling lungs and all.

I thought about the day my two uncles came to our house to take my father away to detox. My mother had enough of the Jekyll and Hyde behavior of my father's drinking, so she called his brothers for some help. They had to tie him down in the bed of a pickup truck because he was kicking and screaming about not wanting to go. "The bottle or your family?" said one of my uncles, and that quieted my father down for a bit.

My father used to use folded matchbook covers to pick food from his teeth, and he used crazy glue to cement his teeth to his gums when they'd fall out. He always carried a bottle of crazy glue in his pocket for when they fell out again. I saw that bottle of glue fall out of his pocket when he struggled with my uncles about being tied down in the truck, and instinctively, I wanted to give it back to him. But I didn't. *Fuck him*, I thought. I was ten at the time.

My father kept booze stashed all over the house—a pint in his recliner chair, a bottle in the back of the linen closet, all sorts of nips and quarts and beer cans under the cellar stairs—and I used to hide under those stairs with the dust and the bugs when he'd come home drunk and angry, falling all over himself. I used to lie to the people around town about my father's drinking—my teachers and coaches and neighbors—but they knew who he was without me trying to hide it. I told my uncles to tie him down good that day.

I knew there was a hiker not far ahead of me. I couldn't see them, but I could sense them. I could tell by the way the leaves were turned over and scattered along the trail because they were wet in spots, unlike the other leaves. I could see more defined boot prints, and I knew somebody was close by. I would catch them.

I felt a surge of adrenaline that wasn't there just moments before. My legs suddenly felt stronger, and my breathing became more constant and steadier. My rhythm was back. I could feel the look on my face change, as I became more focused on the task at hand. My toddler-sized steps became manly steps, and I began to thrust myself up the rock face. My painful grunts turned into determined grunts, and I felt stronger and hungrier. Suddenly, I felt like one of those football players my father used to speak of on

Sunday afternoons. I knew that I would catch that hiker in front of me. It was only a matter of time.

I could see him now. I was gaining ground at a steady pace, and he didn't know I was behind him. I could smell his sweat, and I could hear his staggered breathing. I used that as more fuel to reach him. The fire in my belly was burning through my skin, and I could feel the streams of sweat rolling down my face. My calves burned. My chest pounded. I could almost reach out and touch him. I readied myself to pass him. He knew I was right behind him. He turned to see. He said hello as he stepped to the side. I said hello back, as I trudged onward.

I caught him. I reeled him in. But I must keep going. I must reach the summit with the same pace I used to track him down. I needed to be sitting on the summit, pack removed, by the time he got there. That was my job, and my father would certainly call me a ball player if he could see me now.

His name was Red Dog, and he reached the summit of Swim Bald just moments after I did. "Hell of a climb," he said, as he dropped his pack on the floor of Sassafras Gap Shelter. "You were moving along at a pretty good clip," he added.

"Yeah," I said, shrugging my shoulders. "If I slowed down, I would've rolled back down the mountain."

He laughed, and we shook hands.

Red Dog was from South Africa, and he had that smooth accent where the words just rolled off his tongue. Silky smooth. He talked about how he researched the Appalachian Trail thoroughly before he jumped on a plane to come and hike it. He had soft yellow hair, broad shoulders, and profound cheekbones. He talked about his girlfriend back home and about missing her like crazy. I laughed in response, and I told him about Jada back in Florida. He laughed when I told him about the phone call I made to her at work and how I acted like some pissed-off customer. He shook his head and said his girl would've killed him if he ever did that to her.

Red Dog said he was committed to reaching Harper's Ferry, West Virginia, but then he would reevaluate to see if he wanted to keep hiking to Maine. I nodded my head, as if I agreed with his plan, but on the inside, I just couldn't understand how only going halfway was an option for him. It would be like the football player who only committed to playing half the game, or the marathon runner who only planned for thirteen point one miles. I just nodded my head as Red Dog spoke, and then I said something funny about how I was reevaluating my time on the trail every day. He laughed at that.

It had been several days since I'd seen Leif or Radar or Mr. B, and I wondered if I had seen the last of them. The only way I could see them catching up to me was if I took an extended rest somewhere. The logbook in Sassafras Gap Shelter let us know that there were a few hikers within a couple days of us, but we had no idea who was coming up from behind. Maybe there were other hikers right on our tail? A pair of women hikers calling themselves Turtle and Hare were only a few days ahead of us, and Nomad and Shenandoah were just a day or so ahead of them. I looked forward to meeting those hikers, but Red Dog said he was going to take things slow over the next few days. He was excited to see the Smokey Mountains and wanted to slow his pace so he could see more and do more while he was there. Crazy. I had a twenty-one-mile hike planned for the next day because Fontana Dam and the Smokies awaited, so I figured that might be the last time I got to see Red Dog as well. We stayed up late that night telling stories of where we came from, and both of us mended our blistered heels with moleskin and ate too much granola. He declined a cigarette when I offered him one, but he did pull some chewing tobacco from his pack and started chewing. "My girlfriend would kill me if she knew I was chewing out here," he said, and then I told him about the tobacco-chewing country boy I ran into at Tritt's general store. Red Dog started howling, saying that he met that same kid. "A mouth *full* of chew!" he said, as we both laughed.

My internal alarm started buzzing before the sun came up, and Red Dog kept snoring as I suited up and hiked with the early morning sunrise. I left a note for him in the logbook, wishing him a good and safe hike, and that maybe we'd see one another again down the trail.

I couldn't remember the last time I'd watched the sunrise, so I took my time that morning to see the edges of the sun coming up over the mountain range. I felt warm and content with that sunrise. My breathing was relaxed and calm. Rock and Little Rock flashed through my mind. I thought about the park ranger that first morning at Amicalola Falls and how he pulled up his trousers and breathed in the fresh morning air. I started walking slowly. I thought of Mr. B and "Duke by nine!" I thought of Jada not sleeping naked since I left, and about Robert borrowing twenty bucks from her. I remembered how he wished he could come with me. I said a prayer for Robert that morning under my breath. I looked out at the sunrise over the mountains, and I realized that my insides were in a different place. I felt peaceful. I felt aligned with what I saw around me. I paused at that realization. It must have been the elusive "fellowship with the wilderness" that I read about on top of Springer Mountain. Everything felt easy and simple.

The terrain up and over Cheoah Bald was strenuous, and it brought some doubt about my being able to hike twenty-one miles to Fontana Dam that day. The moleskin I used to patch my heels started to roll up at the edges, and I could feel the bloody moisture in my socks with each step. The bandages started to slip and slide, and the blood in my socks caused a squeaking sound with each step. I was afraid to take my boots off before Fontana, so I pushed on, humming songs to fade out the sounds of my squeaking, bloody feet.

A freshwater spring popped up out of the ground at Cable Gap, and a teenage boy with long, curly brown hair and Velcro sandals knelt in front of the pool rinsing his face. He wore a long-sleeved purple flowered shirt, polyester, buttoned once near the waist, and the water ran down his face and exposed chest when he heard me coming and stood up. "Hey man," he said, with a surprised tone in his voice. "How's it going? I'm Nomad."

I recalled the name from the logbook at Sassafras, but he didn't look much like a hiker to me. "Hey," I said. "How's it going? You're a thru-hiker?"

"Hell, yeah, man. Came out here from Califor-ni-a! Gonna change my name from Nomad to something else though, cuz some other goddamn hiker is already going by Nomad."

"So, what are you changing your name to?" I said, kneeling beside him to fill my water jug.

"Not sure yet, man. Still thinkin' on it. What's your trail name?"

"Bird," I said.

"Bird?" he said as he started flapping his arms in the air. "Any specific kind of bird?"

"Nope," I said. "Just Bird."

"Well, right on, Bird!"

"Yep, right on," I said, standing back up. "You hiking on to Fontana today?" I asked.

"No way, man. Not today. It's getting late, and there's still some five or so miles before Fontana. I'd never get there before the sun goes down," he said. "But I'm stoked to hike through the Smokies, man! Woo-wee!" he shouted. "The Smokies are gonna be awesome, bro!"

"Yeah, pretty exciting stuff," I said. "Well, I'm hiking on to Fontana, so I'll catch up with you later on, Nomad."

"Okay, man. Sounds good. Hey, before you go though, do you have any extra food you can spare? I'm running pretty low on supplies and all, and I could use a little something to get me to the Smokies if you don't mind."

I took a long look at Nomad before I said anything. His eyes looked distant and carefree. His feet and sandals were covered in mud, and the dirt under his fingernails looked permanent. It was the shirt that really got me though—I couldn't see how any hiker would waste their time with a shirt like that. "You got any food at all?" I asked.

"No, not really," he said. "Some granola, but that's about it."

"You got any boots to go along with those sandals?" I asked.

"Nope. This is it, man. These here are my walking shoes."

"You got any money to buy food once you get to Fontana?" I asked.

"Ah, nope. No funds to my name, man. I plan on working a bit here and there as I hike along," he said. "You know, helping a farmer one day and washing dishes in a restaurant the next. I'll do whatever I got to, but no, don't have any funds right now, man."

Part of me wanted to smack him in the face and tell him to get his shit together, but the other part of me wanted to give him all the food I had left in my pack. I asked him what he was doing for a sleeping bag, and he pulled a smaller fleece blanket from his pack. I asked what he was doing for clean water, and he pulled a bottle of iodine tablets from his pocket.

His pack was small and dirty, with a few rips here and there, and he said he was getting his clothes from other hikers who were looking to downsize the loads they were carrying. "I got these here shorts from a guy last week," he said. "Pretty sweet, huh?"

"What about a tent? You got a tent?"

"Nope. No tent, man. But check this out," he said, as he started fishing through his pack. "I got this from a guy back in Neel's Gap a few weeks ago, and I love the thing." He pulled a mesh hammock from his pack, and he told me to hold one side as he backed up and stretched it out. "Pretty sweet, right?"

"Yeah, pretty sweet," I said.

"I sleep like a champ in this thing, man! It's awesome."

Without telling Nomad how I really felt, I reached into my pack and pulled out my food bag. "You got a stove to cook on?" I asked.

He laughed and rolled his eyes. "Man, what kind of hiker would I be if I didn't have a stove? Of course, I have a stove!"

I opened my mouth to respond, but then I took another look at who I was talking to and stopped. I had plenty of supplies to get me to Fontana, so I gave him some rice and cheese and a couple cans of chicken.

"Wow," he said. "Very kind of you, Bird."

"Don't mention it," I replied.

The sun had already set long before I reached Fontana Dam. Talking to Nomad for a while slowed me down some, and the last five miles into Fontana were brutal. Straight up. Straight down. Unforgiving. The trail eventually intersected with Old Highway 28, and I had several miles of pavement to walk in the dark before I reached the Fontana Motel. It was a Friday night in a town of less than one hundred people, so my hopes for a little traffic along the highway and a ride to the motel were quickly dashed. It was dark and quiet, and I could hear the electrical buzz of the streetlights as I walked under them. I started thinking about how heavy my pack was. I started thinking about how nice room service would be. My mouth started watering at the thought of a medium-rare New York strip. I wanted someone to carry me. I wanted Jada to be standing at the bend in the road up ahead. The stars were shining brightly, and the moon was nearly full, but I was thinking about the nasty taste in my mouth and my dirty teeth. I needed a shower and my toothbrush. I needed new moleskin for my heels and a ninety-minute massage. I needed soft sheets and multiple pillows. I needed a cigarette.

After twenty-plus miles of hiking that day, I finally saw the sign for the Fontana Motel. What a welcome sight it was! A big fat smile came to my face, and I no longer thought about my stinky breath and the dirt under my fingernails. All I could think about was a hot shower and water running over my cracked skin. I could almost taste the minty toothpaste being brushed around in my mouth. I thought about Nomad spending the night wrapped up in his fleece blanket, rocking back and forth in his mesh hammock, eating the food I gave him, and I couldn't have felt any more grateful that I had the money to sleep in clean sheets that night. Delightful!

It was nearly nine o'clock at night when I got there, and it was like they knew I was coming. As I approached the front of the motel, there was a man standing there barefoot, smoking a cigarette. When he saw me coming, he threw his cigarette aside and rushed over to me. "Let me take that," he said, reaching for my pack.

I let out a big sigh as I peeled the pack off my shoulders, and he laughed at the sound of my beat body.

"My name is Jeff," he said. "My wife's name is Nancy and we run this place. Happy to have you here," he said.

"You don't know how good it feels to take that pack off," I said. "Sorry I'm getting here so late."

"No need to apologize," he said. "Glad you made it." He shouldered my pack and said, "Follow me. You'll be in room number four tonight, and it's right over here."

I started to follow him before stopping. "Do I need to check in first or give you my credit card or something?"

"Plenty of time for that later," he said. "I'm not looking to rush you or anything like that, but it's a little after nine now, and if you want to go to town to get some supplies, then you'll need to do that now cuz everything closes at ten."

"Man, I couldn't walk another mile today if you paid me, so I'll pass on going into town tonight."

"There's no need for you to walk anywhere," he said. "My wife will gladly take you into town if you want. She'll be out front in a minute or two to drive you, and there's everything you could want in town. Pizza, subs, chips, ready-to-eat meals… Whatever you want," he said.

"Really?" I said. "I'm not looking to put you guys out or anything like that, but…."

"Don't be silly," he said. "Go in and drop your stuff, and then come over to the front lobby, and Nancy will be there to give you a lift. Our pleasure," he said.

"Wow," I said. "Top-notch service, Jeff. I think I'll take you up on that."

Three minutes later, I was getting into the passenger side of Nancy's minivan. She sat behind the idle engine as I buckled my seatbelt and said hello to her. As soon as my door was closed, she sped off. "I'm Nancy," she said.

"I'm Bird," I replied.

"Nice to meet you, Bird. Happy you could join us tonight."

"It's awfully nice of you to be taking me to town like this," I said. "I definitely wasn't expecting it."

"It's all part of the package deal," she said. "You hiking up to Maine?" she asked.

"That's the plan," I said.

I sat quietly for a minute, thinking about the *package deal* she spoke of. I had no idea how much the motel room was going to cost that night, or the taxi ride to town late on a Friday. I was okay with splurging on myself a little bit, but I didn't want to go overboard with spending hundreds of dollars in Fontana Dam. I was worried that Jeff and Nancy were adding all these services up in their heads, and then come checkout time, they'd slam me with some outrageous bill.

"The supermarket is eight miles away," she said, "and I'm happy to wait out front for you while you grab some things. Everything closes soon though, so please excuse me for driving a little fast. Once you get your supplies, I'm happy to swing you by the bank ATM if you want. It's right down the road from the supermarket."

Yep, that's right I thought. She's reeling me in with all these extra services, and I'm gonna pay a pretty hefty price for all this when I check out. "That would be great, Nancy. I appreciate that very much. I'll be quick inside the grocery store."

"As long as we get you there before they close," she said.

Minutes later, Nancy pulled right up to the front of the store and let me out. "I'll be parked right over there," she said, pointing to the spot where all the shopping carts were stored.

It was like the supermarket was expecting me. As soon as I walked in the front door, I was standing in front of a deli station that had so many different selections to choose from. It was the end of the day, so everything from the back kitchen was up front and on display. There were roast beef and ham sandwiches all wrapped up, calzones with red sauce, fried chicken wings, bags of chips, oatmeal cookies, hummus, carrot cakes, and coleslaw. My eyes couldn't handle the sight of all that food, so I took a deep breath and grabbed one of those hand-held plastic carriers. I went right down the line, selecting one of just about everything they had. My mouth couldn't wait to feast on all that food, and I could all but taste the fried chicken just by smelling it. I moved at a quick pace, not really caring about the cost of each item, and within minutes I was paying thirty-seven dollars to the forty-something-year-old cashier woman. "Pretty hungry tonight?" she asked.

"You could say that," I said with a smile.

I saw Nancy smoking in the front seat of her minivan when I came out of the store, and she flicked her cigarette away when I got back into the car. "You didn't have to put that out on my account," I said. "I smoke too."

"Feel free to smoke if you want," she said. "Did you get the fried chicken?" she asked. "They have really good fried chicken."

"Sure did," I said, lighting up a cigarette. "I got a little bit of everything," I said, laughing.

I still had some cash on me, so I passed on going to the ATM, and Nancy drove at a much slower speed on the way back to the motel. "How long have you and Jeff been running the motel?" I asked.

"Oh, I dunno," she said. "Maybe fifteen years. We sure do love this place though, and all the hikers we meet. Every day is a little different, with the different hikers coming through and all."

"Sounds like a good way of life," I said.

"Yeah, we've met some really interesting people along the way," she said, "and every single hiker seems to have their own reasons for being out there on the trail. Some people are young and adventurous. Some are old, not wanting to get older. It's funny how some people think this trail is like the fountain of youth or something. More often than not, this trail makes the old even older. Ain't nothing easy about hiking this trail," she said.

"You got that right," I said.

"Then there are the people who are out here because they're searching for something or because they lost something. We've met lots of people who were recently divorced and some who've lost a loved one. Some people want to find God out here, and then there are others who are nine-to-fivers and just want a little bit of nature for themselves. Everybody's got a different reason for being out here, Bird, so why are you out here? What's your reason?"

"Well, that's a loaded question, Nancy, and if you were a psychiatrist and had fifteen extra hours to spare, I could probably tell you all my reasons for being out here." She and I both laughed. "But the short answer is probably a little bit of everything you just said. I feel like I'm searching for something, but I don't think I know exactly what that something is just yet."

"Sounds like an honest answer, Bird. Honest answer. I hope you find what it is you're looking for."

Nancy pulled into the motel parking lot and put the van in park. I reached into my pocket to pull out some money, and I asked her how much the taxi ride was to the store. "Oh, no, no, no," she said. "We don't have a charge for bringing hikers to the store and to the bank. We don't have a charge for the motel either."

"I'm sorry, what? You don't charge people to stay with you? That doesn't make any sense. How do you guys survive without charging people?"

"We have more of a donation system here," she said, "and we let the people who stay here decide for themselves what they should donate. Some hikers have money to spend and can be generous with their donations, and others who aren't so fortunate, so we let each person donate what they feel is right."

"Wow," I said. "I can't believe that. And you guys are doing okay with that type of setup?"

"Yeah," she said. "We're doing just fine."

"Unbelievable," I said.

"We definitely don't do this for the money though, Bird. Both Jeff and I love meeting all the people, so as long as we can keep this little motel of ours afloat, we feel like the donation setup works best for who we are. If someone doesn't have any money, but they need a warm bed for the night, then we welcome that person just like we would anyone else."

I thought about Nomad and how he'd love their little motel, but a part of me wished he wouldn't come to visit Jeff and Nancy. There was something about Nomad that caused me to think he'd suck Jeff and Nancy dry of all their kindness. I opted not to tell Nancy about Nomad, and I thanked her for the ride to the store and the warm bed to sleep in. "You'll sleep well tonight," she said, "especially after you eat all that fried chicken!"

Room number four had everything a hiker could ever want. The bed was silky and soft with extra pillows, and there was even a fluffy white bathrobe hanging on a hook in the closet. I loved that I could adjust the heat with a simple touch of the finger, and the water pressure in the shower was fantastic. All the simple pleasures that I always took for granted were like small gifts given to me on a Friday night in Fontana.

After a nice long shower, I slid into that bathrobe and dug into my fried chicken. Nancy was right—that chicken was super tasty. My plastic fork went from chicken to coleslaw to carrot cake, then back again. I ate with my fingers too and didn't stop until I couldn't eat any more. Stuffed Bird! With greasy fingers and lips and cheeks and forearms, I decided to take another shower, and I laughed at my ability to do so. Amazing.

The TV in the corner of the room was small, but it had all the basic cable channels. My eyes were tired, and my feet were raw, so I propped my legs up and flipped through the channels. I stopped on CNN because they were reporting on a recent mass shooting in Phoenix, Arizona. They said it was a hate crime and a race crime. Some white guy apparently walked into a minority supermarket and opened fire on the people inside. They showed some footage of the police cars in front of the store, and then they interviewed one of the store employees and called the guy a hero for trying to protect his co-workers. They also interviewed an eight-year-old girl who was in the store at the time of the shooting, and she said she wasn't scared for herself, but that she was scared for her mother. Crazy.

Then CNN had a Zoom interview with a white female professor who was *qualified* to speak on this type of crime, and she went on to say that this was an example of white supremacy and how white people were now more willing to act on their desires. "They want to hold onto white power in this country," she said.

That professor, who looked safe and sound in her nice suburban bedroom someplace, went on to say that certain white people were growing more and more concerned about holding onto their authentic white bloodlines. Certain whites haven't liked the mixing of races they see happening in society, and they are afraid that more browns and blacks and mixed races would only diminish the overall white footprint in this country and in the world.

I clicked the TV off and sat in the silence of room number four for a while. W*hat the fuck?* I recalled a conversation I had with Robert a couple months after we became friends, and he was telling me about what it was like to be half-black in America. He said it was all fucked up how, in certain white settings, he acted whiter, but in all black settings, he acted all black. "I'm not sure why that is," he said, "but it's the truth." He said it's taken him his entire life to try and figure out who he was at his core, but that he still wasn't quite sure.

Robert told me about a book he had read a few years earlier by Ta-Nehisi Coates called *Between the World and Me,* and he said that if I wanted to know more about the black experience in America, then I should take a look at that book. And I did. I read that book, and it was powerful and raw. I learned a lot from that book, but to be honest, I only read it because Robert was my friend, and I wanted to keep him as a friend. He asked me to read it, so I did because I wanted to show him what his friendship meant to me. Sure, I learned some things about black culture and white supremacy from reading that book, but I didn't pick it up on my own. I needed him to tell me about it.

I knew that if Robert and I were ever going to be friends in the society of today, then I needed to tell him exactly how I felt about the issue of race. It wasn't a secret that Robert protected his black lineage more than his white, he told me so, and I appreciated his honesty about that, so I knew I needed to be completely honest with him about who I was as a white man in America. And that book by Coates was one way for us to have a discussion about race. Robert would talk about certain sections of that book that stood out to him, and I would do the same thing. Robert pointed to the section of the book that talked about the inner-city streets of Baltimore and the black-on-black crime that existed there, and I talked about the sections of that book that grouped the beliefs of all white people together. Robert talked about how he believed that the oppression enforced by whites on blacks had a continuous generational effect and that blacks didn't have the same opportunities as whites, even if the laws suggested that they might. I talked to Robert about how I thought it was bold of Coates to say that *all* white people were power hungry and that our primary purpose was to dominate and control the black people around us. "That's just not me," I said to Robert, "and a part of me takes offense when Coates puts me in that same category with all the other white people. Coates doesn't even know me," I said.

"Well," said Robert, "Coates doesn't know me either, but do you agree with what he says about the past oppressions that still have an effect on present day African Americans?"

"I agree that the path for the black person in this country is more challenging than the path for the white person, so yes, I would agree with that. But do you think it's fair that Coates puts every white person in the same group when he talks about the central inherited belief of the white person is to dominate and exclude the African American?"

"I'm not sure," said Robert. "But I will say that I instinctively feel a need to protect myself as a black man in this country, and I don't feel that way about my white side. I just feel more at home when I'm in a group of black people rather than a group of white people."

"But the color of your skin is more black," I said. "Do you think that plays a role in why you feel that way?"

"Yeah, of course," he said. "If my skin were more white, I'd probably feel more white, and more comfortable around white people. But my skin isn't white, and that's the first thing white people see when they meet me. They see a light-colored black man… and I've always felt the need to protect that."

"So, do you think I view you merely as a black man and that I instinctively want to dominate you and exclude you?"

"Not yet," he said.

"Not yet?" I replied.

"White people have let me down time and time again," he said. "At first, they appear one way, but more is always revealed as time goes on, man."

"So, does that mean you're on a *wait-and-see* basis with our friendship?"

"Isn't it always that way?" he said.

"Hmm," I replied. "I don't have those same types of reservations about you and our friendship."

"It's cuz you're white," he said…

Suddenly, I felt like an absolute stranger to myself in room number four. I was in a small town that I didn't know, meeting and talking to people I didn't know, lying on a mattress that wasn't mine, wrapped in a warm robe that wasn't mine, and the feeling came over me that I didn't know who I was. The silence in that room grew louder around midnight, and I started questioning everything. What was my purpose in life? What were my reasons for being out here on this trail? Why was I in this strange place? What was I searching for? What mattered to me?

I never viewed Robert as either black or white because that never mattered to me. I liked Robert because he was from the same place as me and he spoke the same language. We both struggled in this world, we both made shitty decisions in the past, but we were both in a position where we were trying to be better men. We both wanted more out of life, more out of ourselves, and that's what I liked about him. I liked that we were both trying to swim upstream and make something more out of our lives. It was never a black or white thing for me, and I never questioned whether our friendship would last because of the different colors of our skin. But was that me being naive? It was something that

Robert was obviously aware of, cautious of, skeptical about, and I wondered if those reservations prevented him from really being able to open up to me, like he might with another black person. If he instinctively felt a need to protect his 'blackness' from me, then how could we ever be friends, true friends, in this world? If he was always thinking about when I'd *change* into all the other white people, then why would he even try to be my friend?

One of the interesting observations I made about that Coates book was when Coates himself befriended a couple white co-workers for the first time. It was interesting that, in a book that stereotyped white people as domineering over blacks, that Coates himself talked about the good relationships he had with the first white people he met. Maybe Robert was like Coates in that sense? Maybe Robert was optimistic about the possibility of a friendship where race didn't matter?

When I first got sober, I was scared to death. I knew I had a problem with drinking and drugging, and I really didn't think I'd be able to stop. I hated looking back over the decisions I made in my life when I was all fucked up, and nothing I did could get that shameful taste out of my mouth. I was grateful for the men who took me under their wings and talked to me about their own struggles. They talked to me about the shit they used to do when they were drunk and all banged up, but then they talked to me about how they were able to stop it all. They were able to quit the booze and the drugs, and they told me that I could do it too, but only if I made the effort. And even though I appreciated the time those men took to talk to me, I was still scared, and I still doubted my ability to stop.

But then, thirty days of sobriety turned into sixty days, and one year turned into two. Slowly but surely, the obsession and the cravings to drink and use drugs diminished, and I found myself in a place where I no longer thought about using drugs every day. The men who came before me called it a miracle. They told me that I was one of a few who were able to solve the drink and drug problem, but they also said the only way I could stay clean was if I turned around and gave it away to the next person who was still suffering. So I did, and that's how I became friends with Robert. I had two years clean when I met him, and he was still in that dark place of not thinking he could make it. I took the time out of my day to sit with Robert and talk with him about my past and the things I had to do to stop using. Our friendship grew quickly, or so I thought, and I knew our friendship was one of the priceless things that helped keep me sober. I valued our friendship, and I thought he did too. *Damn.*

But borrowing twenty dollars from a friend is never a good sign for a drug addict, and when Jada told me about Robert borrowing money from her, I had a feeling that things weren't good for Robert.

I wasn't all that surprised when Jada told me the news, but it sure was sad to hear her say it. After a much-needed Friday night at the Fontana Motel with my new friends Jeff and Nancy, I decided to call Jada before I left that place. Her voice sounded cracked and bruised, and it was only a matter of moments before she told me what I guess I already suspected. She told me that they found Robert's body in his apartment that Friday afternoon. He never showed up to work the day before, or the day before that, and when his co-workers couldn't reach him, one of them stopped by his place to check on him. The drugs were still on the table. Fentanyl they said. He had collapsed on the tiled floor of his kitchen. His light-colored black skin had turned purple by the time they found him.

Black or white just didn't seem to matter anymore, and I thanked Jada for telling me the news. "But I can't talk about this right now," I said to her. "I'll give you a call the next time I reach a phone."

"I'm so sorry," she said. "I love you."

"Yeah, me too," I replied.

9:02pm

Our family has never been known for staying sober, so it was bittersweet to read about Andy finding his sobriety. I don't remember the day my uncles tied my father down in the bed of a pickup truck; I must've been too young to remember. I wasn't shocked to read about it though. I do remember the crazy glue, however, and the times our father's teeth would fall out of his mouth.

Andy never mentioned Robert to me before, and I have mixed feelings about that. On one hand, I'm glad Andy had a friend like that in Robert, but on the other hand, I feel like that friend should have been me.

8

My heels felt good as I walked away from the Fontana Motel, but my pack felt heavy. My heart felt heavy too, and that just made everything heavy. I saw Nomad walking toward the motel as I was walking away from it, and I felt bad for Jeff and Nancy. I wondered if Nancy would offer him a free ride to the supermarket, and I wondered how long Nomad would take advantage of their *donation* policy. He and I talked briefly as we passed one another on the road, and Nomad said something about one of his sandals breaking. "Gonna have to get me some new walking shoes," he said.

"Good luck with that," I said, knowing that he wasn't getting his hands on my boots.

"Hey, thanks again for that food, man. It was great."

"Don't mention it," I replied.

I couldn't help but think of Robert as I walked along. I didn't know many details surrounding his death, but I knew that heroin laced with fentanyl was the cause that created the outcome. Robert was gone, and all I could think about was what might have brought him to the point of sticking the needle in his arm again. He said he wanted to come along with me on the hike, and I started kicking myself for not making that happen. Why didn't I make that happen? He'd still be alive if he came along, right? I thought about that Bill Bryson book, *A Walk in the Woods*, and the part where the old acquaintance, Katz, asked Bryson if he could tag along for the hike. Bryson didn't want to hike with Katz, but he ended up taking him along anyway, and that whole story is about the bond those two guys created out on the trail. So, why didn't I seek that same sort of connection with Robert? Did he feel like I didn't want him to come along?

Making the decision to use drugs again after a period of sobriety has been one of my greatest fears, and I wondered what Robert felt the moment before he injected that needle. Was the addict in him just too strong for the sober guy he was trying to be? I wondered what that must have been like—what that must have felt like. Did he want to die more than he wanted to live? Was he simply looking to escape? I mean, he knew that using again meant giving up, so why did he just give in and quit like that?

I wanted to get the taste of Robert's death out of my mouth, but I couldn't. I ate granola and drank water, but the taste of him being purple and lifeless and dead was still there. I smoked cigarettes and thought about seeing Jada again, but those smoky thoughts of my girlfriend somehow added to the vision of Robert's motionless body lying dead on the tiled floor of his kitchen. My brain started working overtime as memories of Robert flooded my ability to see anything else. I forced myself to think about watching a baseball game or making love to Jada, but I just couldn't get away from those thoughts of Robert. If I could've done anything to escape, I would have.

My brain was tired, but I was well rested. I could see how the primitive way of life on the trail had begun to grow on me like my beard, but I didn't want to follow a path and climb rocks that day. I wanted to escape. I didn't want to feel it anymore. I craved a distraction. I wanted to get dressed for work and listen to music as I drove in my car. I wanted to wash my clothes and listen to the spin cycle while watching TV on the couch. I wanted to spend money on coffee and cigarettes, and I wanted to cook a nice meal in my kitchen. I wanted to do anything except climb rocks. I wanted to taste anything except the memory of Robert. I needed a new taste.

I had never seen an actual dam before, but I could see Fontana Dam up ahead. I could see how the trail had me walking across the top of it. That massive concrete slab wedged between two mountain ranges had to be at least a thousand feet tall, and it was something else to look at. As I made my way on top of it, I wondered how long it would take to build something that massive. On the left side of the dam was a huge lake with calm waters and quiet shorelines; to the right was a tremendous drop-off, at least a thousand feet down, with small waterfalls spitting out from the center of the concrete slab. I stood on top of that structure for a while and tried to calculate the time and manpower needed for a job like that. Man could build a structure like that... but man could also jump from a structure like that. Man could triumph in those types of accomplishments... but man could also quit and throw himself over the edge.

Thoughts of joining Robert in the next life didn't frighten me, but the idea that one step to my right would accomplish it did frighten me. I didn't want to die, but I did want to talk to my friend again. I didn't want to jump, but I'd be lying if I said I wasn't thinking about it. I could see myself jumping. Honestly, I could. I could feel the free fall before impact. I could sense the sudden blackness immediately after crashing into the rocks—my world would turn black. All my whiteness would immediately turn black. I thought about my friend more as I contemplated the difference between our whiteness and blackness. I wasn't sure I would ever know how he felt before sticking that needle back in his arm.

"Afternoon," said a voice from behind me. "Great view, huh?"

"Holy shit!" I said, turning around. "You scared me half-to-death," I said, to a scruffy, middle-aged guy wearing a flannel shirt and a yellow construction hat.

"Sorry 'bout that," he said. "Didn't mean to scare ya. Just saw you out here with your pack on and thought I'd say hello. You headed up to Maine?"

"Yeah," I said. "Maine. That's the plan."

"I've thought about hiking this here trail many times myself, but never have. Is it worth all the hype?"

"Um, yeah," I said. "I'd say it's worth it. It's different from what I expected, but yeah, it's worth it."

"Yeah, maybe someday," he said. "If the wife lets me and all." He laughed. "I see lots of hikers cross over the dam this time of year, and every time I see one of'm, I just wanna drop everything and tag along with'm."

"Well, I hope one day you do that," I said. "Sounds like you might regret it if you don't."

"I'm Spence," he said, sticking out his hand. "Spence Hawkins."

I shook his hand. "Hello, Spence. I'm Bird. You work here on the dam?"

"Yeah, I've been working this dam for nearly twelve years now."

"Long time," I said.

"Yeah, it's been a while. But, like I said, I just wanted to say hello and make sure you were alright. I saw you out here looking over the edge for a while, and I just wanted to make sure things were okay."

"Well," I said. "I appreciate that, Spence. I'm just taking my time and soaking up everything this view has to offer."

You know, you can call it whatever you want, but I have a hard time viewing Spence's coming over to me as some sort of coincidence. I mean, I was deep in thought in a place where it's never advised to be that deep in thought, and Spence seemed to show up at the exact time I needed someone to help pull my head out of my ass. I mean, I was missing Robert something bad that day, and I sure am grateful that Spence checked in on me and interrupted the conversation I was having with my dead friend. I don't know what to call it, but you can call it a coincidence if you want. I think Spence knew I was taking in more than just the view.

I had heard some things about the Smoky Mountains, but the main thing I heard was that the bears were pretty tame throughout the park and didn't mind being around people. I was looking forward to hiking through that stretch of mountains, but it was springtime, and I wasn't looking forward to any encounters with hungry bears. My plan was to keep all my food sealed up in Ziplock bags and then hang my food in trees before I went to bed. Sure, I wanted to see a bear but not because one was chasing me for my granola and cheese.

It wasn't a bear that first caused me to pause in the Smoky Mountains though, it was a flier posted to a tree. I had already seen several fliers posted to trees along the trail, but this one was different. This one said:

BEWARE!
Armed and dangerous fugitives are believed to be hiding out on this section of the Appalachian Trail. Please take caution around strangers and call 911 to report any suspicious behavior. Thank you and be safe.

Immediately, I started thinking about all the people I had met on the trail up to that point, and the only person I could think of that was suspicious in any way was that cross-legged army guy smoking weed in the corner of Spring Shelter. I started thinking more about that guy and the pissed-off way about him, but then I was stopped, yet again, by another flier posted on another tree. This one featured a photo of two female hikers in their twenties kneeling with a golden retriever. They had big smiles on their faces, and they were strapped into their packs, but the caption went on to say that these were the last two people to go missing in the Smoky Mountain region, and if anyone had any information, to call the authorities.

I wasn't too scared or spooked to keep hiking, but I was suddenly very aware of everything around me. The woods became extremely quiet that day, and the sound of the wind blowing or a tree branch bending or a twig snapping, caused me to stop, process, and dismiss before moving on. I became hypersensitive to any sound or movement, and even though I didn't like those feelings of something closing in on me, I was grateful that this new feeling pulled me away from thinking about Robert.

The trail dragged on and on that day, and the hiking never seemed to end. And here's the thing: I've never had any issues walking places, like to the beach or to the store. But my 'walks' have always ended on the same day they started. You know what I mean? So, this six-month 'walk' just seemed to drag on and on, never with an end in sight. It was the type of walk that played tricks on my thinking—the type of walk where thinking about the end of the walk wasn't really suggested. If I started thinking about the end of the walk, I would get overwhelmed with the reality that I still had nineteen hundred miles to go. And that was a brutal thought! I'd quit in less than a week if I kept thinking about that. Brutal. *One day at a time* I kept telling myself.

Sometimes, in the mornings, I would put my finger on the place on the map where I was, and at the end of the day, my finger would still be in the same place. And I hated that feeling. This was the type of walk where I couldn't think about the walk because if I did, then I would go crazy with the fact that it never fucking ended! Because when I looked at the map at the end of the day and I put my finger on where I was, it felt like I never moved. Insane. But I did move, and it was hard work to hike fifteen miles in a day, so when I'd look at the map at the end of the day, it always looked like I was in the exact same place before. Crazy.

I found my thoughts going from Robert to bears to killers hiding out in the wood, and then it would start all over again—Robert, bears, killers in the woods. I had to get off the emotional rollercoaster spinning through my brain, but the trail just kept right on going, up and down, over and under, no end in sight. And my mind kept churning right along with it.

I'm not sure when it happened, but I started thinking about my early days of sobriety. I thought about how hard it was to stay sober on a *one day at a time* basis. I mean, life was tough, and every day seemed to throw different shit my way. But I started to think about how I navigated through all that crap and stayed sober. I started thinking about all the people who helped me get through those tough times, and there were many.

Her name was Mo, and I only knew her because she went to the same meetings that I went to. It's not that Mo was pretty and sexy and had what I wanted; in fact, it was just the opposite. Mo spent her life in a wheelchair because she had many different deformities that kept her from walking. Mo didn't have arms like most people do; she had smaller knobs that acted like arms, and at the end of each knob were small ball-shaped fingers. Mo couldn't really use her arms like other people, but her wheelchair was designed so she could steer with one of her finger knobs. Mo didn't have legs either, like most people do, because her legs ended where my knees are. She did have little feet though, but her legs weren't the kind of legs that could be used for walking. On top of that, Mo had issues with her skin and the structure of her head. She had dark port-wine stains over a huge portion of her face, and she couldn't hold her head straight on her shoulders; it was always slanted to the right.

The one thing Mo did have was a smile, and it was big and contagious. I remember the day Mo celebrated four years of continuous sobriety, and it was something else to see. I had about a year clean myself, and when they handed out coins that day, I watched Mo as she zoomed herself up to get her four-year medallion. Mo couldn't talk all that well, but that day, the room fell completely silent as she spoke about how grateful she was to be alive and sober. I sat in awe, as she talked about her wonderful experiences as a sober woman.

Later that afternoon, after Mo picked up her medallion, I went to lunch with a friend of mine named Ronnie. He had been at the meeting with me earlier, and we talked about Mo picking up her coin. He said, "You know, you and I have the ability to get out of bed every morning and go to work. You and I have the ability to drive our cars and fall in love. You and I have the ability to hold hands with our partners, have sex, and walk on the beach, but those are all things that Mo will never do. She will never walk on the beach like we do. She will never have sex like we do. She will never go to work like we do, or walk down the street, or drive a car. But even still, she is sober, and she is grateful for the life she lives."

I don't know why I started thinking about Mo that day in the Smoky Mountains, but I'm glad I did. Yes, I was pissed and hurt and saddened by the news of my friend, Robert. Yes, I was scared and spooked about some maniac jumping out of the woods to murder me. Yes, I was nervous about the encounter with a bear I hadn't seen yet, but through all of that, I still had the ability to think about Mo. And when I compared my life to the life of Mo, I realized that there really wasn't a comparison. When I thought about how grateful Mo was the day she picked up her medallion,

I realized that I had nothing, absolutely nothing, to complain about. No, I didn't like the fact that my brain had so much freedom to think about whatever it wanted to on the trail, but I was grateful that my thoughts went to positive experiences after the negative ones. Yes, I will miss Robert, but that doesn't mean I have to go to that dark place with him. Yes, those woods scared me, but at least I had the ability to experience them in their fullness, unlike my friend Mo.

In high school, Andy used to borrow old man Johnson's car without him knowing. My brother used to sneak out of our house late at night and walk across the neighborhood to Mr. Johnson's place. The driver's side door of his car was always unlocked, and Johnson always kept the keys in the glove box, probably so he'd never lose them. The tank was always full of gas, and my brother would joyride around town with his buddies all night before returning the car to Johnson's place in the morning with an empty tank.

Old man Johnson must've gone nuts time and again with the thoughts of having filled the tank before going home, but my brother always returned it empty. I remember when old man Johnson died, and my brother was pissed when that car went away.

I have a hard time picturing Andy as a sober guy. I never thought he was gonna change. I always pictured him in jail or ending up like our father, or Robert.

9

April Fools' Day came and went without my realizing it. I did, however, realize that everything around me was starting to transform. The April temperatures were warmer than March, and the air tasted a little thinner. The earth itself was turning different shades of green before my eyes, and the birds started humming a different tune. Small patches of life were pushing their way up between rocks and roots, and the curlicue fern buds were starting to straighten out and reach for the sun. The naked forest trees started to show signs of life as little buds inched their way through the branch limbs.

Nature wasn't the only thing changing. I couldn't believe it when the first shelter I came across in the Smokies was jam-packed with vacationers and amateur hikers out for a stay in the woods. There were fathers and sons, couples, old people, even a group of teenagers, and they were all set up for camping around Birch Spring Shelter. It looked like an overcrowded stay in my childhood campground at Myles Standish because clothes lines were hanging from tree to tree, tents were pitched on any clear spot, hiking boots were scattered all around, and the noise from all the people sounded like a swarming group of black flies. A fire roared in the pit as strangers sat around talking and laughing, drinking coffee and beer from styrofoam cups. Little kids were tossing balls back and forth, and two older women were stirring soup and beans in pots over the fire. I removed my pack and sat on a nearby tree stump as I ate granola and watched the overflowing sea of humanity in front of me. People said hello and asked me some basic questions. "Yes, I'm a thru-hiker," I'd say. And, "Yeah, it's a long way to Maine," I'd tell them. And, "Nope, I haven't seen any bears yet."

They were friendly people, but there were just too many of them. I was glad I wasn't spending the night at Birch Spring, and after my snack of some granola and a Snickers, I was happy to strap myself back into my pack and push on.

My plan was to stay in Mollies Ridge Shelter that night, and I hoped and prayed that there would be space inside the shelter for me to sleep. I didn't care so much about a lot of people being there, but I didn't want to go through the process of having to pitch my tent after ten hours of hiking. It didn't take too long to set up the tent, but the next morning the tent would always be damp and heavy, and I hated that. I sure as hell wasn't interested in carrying around a wet tent the next day. Every pound mattered.

It was later in the evening when I arrived at Mollies Ridge, and to my surprise, the only people there were Chillkoot, Saluki, and Red Dog. I wasn't sure when or how they passed me on the trail, it must've been while I was at the Fontana Motel, but it sure was nice to see them rather than all the amateurs and vacationers.

Mollies Ridge must have been deep enough into the Smokies to keep the vacationers away. I didn't have to pitch my tent, and the four of us told stories, ate dinner, patched our heels, and told dirty jokes around the fire. The mood was light and carefree, and even though I thought a lot about Robert that night, I didn't mention anything about him to those guys. I'd laugh when the conversation was funny, and I'd comment this way or that way about a story being told, but the story that occupied my mind that night was one I kept to myself.

I slept in the corner of the shelter that night next to Saluki. I was curious about his trail name, and he told me it was the mascot of the college he went to in Illinois. He said a few other things about his school, but it wasn't long before he yawned real big and rolled over and fell asleep. Everyone fell asleep quickly that night, but I laid there, wide awake with sore knees and hips. I missed the comfort of the Fontana Motel, and I couldn't get settled on the hardwood floor of the shelter. Red Dog started to snore, and I couldn't handle that, so I unzipped my bag, grabbed my smokes and journal, and went to sit out by the fire pit. The fire was gone by that time, but the embers were still red and twinkling, so I smoked my Marlboros as the heat from the coals warmed my feet. I thought about Jada and the warmth I'd feel lying next to her in bed. I closed my eyes and pretended to put myself in bed next to her. I imagined that the heat from those coals was the heat from her body.

I woke up to sunbeams staring at me through the tree limbs, and Red Dog was still snoring. I wasn't sure when I went to bed or how long I slept for, but I felt rested and warm and ready for another day. Chillkoot and Saluki started to come to life, as I finished my early morning coffee and tied the laces of my boots. "Has he been snoring like that all night?" asked Saluki.

"Sure has," I said. "I'll see you guys later on," I said, hoisting up my pack.

The shelters throughout the Smoky Mountains were only five miles apart, so by early afternoon I had already passed by two of them. I was used to only passing one shelter a day, so passing two of them by noon tricked me into thinking I was covering more ground than I was. Ten miles seemed like twenty somehow. The green of the forest floor seemed thicker than it was just a day earlier, and suddenly, without any warning, the trees disappeared, and the trail just opened up to a section of rolling hillsides and vast fields of tall grass. The exposed roots and jagged stones within the dense forest suddenly turned into a narrow dirt walking path with the occasional smooth rock that was discolored with patches of moss. The walking became simple through that stretch, and I could see the horizon out in front with mountain ranges that carried on for miles. The sky was massive without all the trees obstructing my view—it was refreshing to see that much blue. I had to stop for a minute so I could take it all in. I couldn't believe how quickly the landscape changed.

Double Spring Shelter was empty when I arrived. The sun was nearly set, and I wondered if I would have the shelter to myself that night. The shelter was nothing more than a wooden floor with three walls and an open front, and thick patches of rye grass surrounded the shelter. I dropped my pack onto the hardwood floor, and I knelt in the grass and ran my fingers through the soft strands. It felt light and soft and fragile, too good not to lie down in, so I spread myself out on that fresh green patch and rolled around in it. The strands tickled my bare skin, and the earth below the grass was moist and cool.

I remembered how, as a boy, I would run and play in the woods behind our house. I remembered the carefree jumping and skipping and singing. I remembered the rocks, roots, and leaves and how I examined and played in all of it. And then I remembered that I wasn't a kid anymore, but a grown man in my mid-twenties, and I was rolling around in a patch of grass like I was still a boy. What would Red Dog or Saluki say if they came up on me rolling around in the grass like I was? The simple fact was that I had been transported back to my childhood, playing in the soft grassy woods again, and after I had my fill of rolling around, I got up, sat on the hardwood floor of the shelter, and fired up a cigarette. I inhaled and exhaled, and then I felt like an adult again.

I was alone in the shelter that night, and it was peaceful to listen to the wind and the shaking tree limbs. I heard all sorts of sounds that I hadn't heard before, like the scratching and grunting of nearby rodents looking for food. I sat by the fire for several hours before bed, and I ate two helpings of chicken and rice. I thought about spreading my sleeping bag out for the night on that patch of soft grass, but I didn't.

Clingman's Dome is the highest point along the Appalachian Trail, and I had mixed emotions about climbing that mountain. My knee was still sore from the day before, and the uphill climb was rugged and bumpy. The summit of that mountain was unlike the other mountains because Clingman's Dome is a hot spot for tourists and sightseers. I was excited to reach the summit, but that excitement was short-lived and interrupted by camper vans, RVs, paved roads, picnic tables, and too many people. One of the first things I saw on the summit was a big RV with a bumper sticker on the back that said, *This RV climbed Mt. Washington.*

It was early afternoon on the summit, so that meant it was lunchtime, and the picnic tables were full of people eating sandwiches and mothers shouting "mayo or mustard?" to kids who were running and playing. Fathers had frustrated looks on their faces as they tried to gather everyone around for the family photo on top of the mountain. Little kids were slurping sodas and picking their noses, and grandmothers were sitting under the shade of umbrellas and canopies. I tried to embrace the view on top of that mountain because it really was beautiful, but I got caught up in watching a little boy chase his sister around with a big bug in his hand. She screamed bloody hell, and he laughed and laughed as he chased her. "Cut that out, Billy!" screamed a mother from somewhere behind me.

Clingman's Dome let me down—the highest peak on the Appalachian Trail—I was hoping it would feel like more of an accomplishment. Even though I enjoyed the sight of little Billy chasing his sister around, I would have preferred more patches of rye grass, no paved roads, and fewer picnic tables. It was just too easy for people to get to the top of that mountain.

My left knee buckled and flexed a few times on the descent off the Dome, and I popped a couple of Advil while praying for the pain to go away. Mount Love was the only obstacle standing between me and Mount Collins Shelter, so I huffed and I puffed and I limped my way up and over that peak. By the time I reached the shelter, my knee was swollen and pounding. I was tired and beaten up, and I was thinking I might need to take a day off to rest my knee.

It's called *Trail Magic,* and it usually happens when hikers least expect it. It's as if the Gods of the forest know when hikers are suffering, and random gifts or pleasantries are granted to make the hard times a little less hard for those who suffer. I heard a few hikers speak of such magic, but it hadn't happened to me, and I tended to brush off such childish things. I never believed in magic growing up, but then I arrived at Mount Collins Shelter, and that's where I met Old Smoky and Long Way—that's when the magic happened.

Old Smoky was a chubby man, in his late fifties, with a gray beard and a red bandana wrapped tightly around his head. He wore thick glasses that doubled the size of his eyes when you looked at him. Long Way, on the other hand, was tall, thin, and talkative. He was from Maine, maybe thirty, and he said something about taking the *long way* home. The two men were relaxed with boots off, stretching out with legs crossed, and they laughed back and forth as I took off my pack and joined them. And that's when Old Smoky reached into his pack and pulled out a big bag of Taco Bell and said, "Trail magic!"

He must have had fifteen tacos in that bag, and he took a few out for himself before passing it over to Long Way, then to me. "Help yourself," he said. "They might even still be warm."

"Ah, man," said Long Way. "I never dreamed I'd get a couple tacos out here."

"Wow," I said. "Very kind of you, Smoky."

It was magic because a greasy, soft taco had never tasted so delicious. It was magic because the ground beef just melted in my mouth as the spicy flavor burst into the back of my throat. Cheese and lettuce never felt so silky and crisp. Tomatoes never looked so red. Heaven for a hungry hiker! Two tacos weren't enough to fill me, and I resisted grabbing a third, even though Smoky wouldn't have cared if I did. I just sat back and licked the greasy juices from my fingers and thought about all those little things I always took for granted, including greasy tacos from fast food joints. Trail magic!

I thought it would only be the three of us in the shelter that night, but after the sun was down and we were snug in our sleeping bags, we saw the light of a headlamp approaching as it bounced its way toward the shelter. I enjoyed the anticipation because you never knew who was going to step out from behind the light, and that night it was Saluki. He had taken some time to relax earlier in the day, so he pulled into camp late that night, and the three of us slid our gear over to give him some space on the shelter floor. Old Smoky offered him a cold taco, and without hesitation, Saluki accepted and inhaled the magic. The four of us laughed and told stories of the trail for some time that night, and I managed to fall asleep before anyone started snoring.

I woke up earlier than usual the next morning, and I wasn't sure why. I didn't feel all that rested, but I was awake and thinking about coffee. It was still dark, and I knew I could have slept more, but I figured I'd be wide awake once I drank a cup and started hiking. I had a long day of hiking planned, over twenty miles, and getting an early start just meant finishing my day with enough time to eat and relax and get a prime sleeping spot in the next shelter.

The hiking that day was easy, without many ups and downs, but I was troubled by the thoughts of a dream I knew I had the night before. I've always hated knowing I had a dream but not being able to remember who or what it was about. And it was brutal that day because I could taste that dream on the tip of my tongue, but I couldn't remember what it was about. I was hopeful that, at some point in the day, I would see something or hear something that would trigger my memory of that dream, and then BAM! I'd remember everything. But that didn't happen, and I squandered much of that day thinking and hoping that the dream would somehow come back to me.

I took a break and had a smoke early that afternoon. I had thirteen miles left to hike, and the clouds overhead were dark, getting darker. I knew I was going to get wet, so I smoked and I snacked and I finished the cold coffee I had left over from the morning. It wasn't long before the rain started, and my pace became slow and heavy. Even though my pack had a water-resistant covering, the clothes I was wearing didn't, and once the rain came, I got wet, and so did the trail. And once the trail got wet, it got muddy, and that's when everything slowed down, almost to a halt. Slipping and sliding in the mud was unavoidable when the rain came, and tripping or sliding or falling down could have nightmarish consequences for a hiker. My knee was still sore from the day before, my pack was heavier than normal, and who knows what would happen if I went crashing down in the mud?

I started thinking about my father again, and my thoughts of him were slow, like the muddy trail I walked on. I wasn't sure why he came to mind again, but he was there, and that's who I thought about.

My father was an engineer. He was a smart man, but he was the type of man that wouldn't put up with little boys chasing their sisters around the top of Clingman's Dome. My father wouldn't think to ask about mustard or mayo; he would just put whatever he wanted on the sandwich. He was the type of man who would try to kick everyone off the summit of Clingman's Dome so he could have his own private moment on top. My father wasn't the type of man who would bring his work home with him, and he never talked to us kids about the things he did to fill his days. He would leave early in the morning for work, and then he would come home late at night, drunk more times than not. He never talked to us about the work he did to put food on the table, and he never asked us what we wanted to be when we got older. He was a quiet man in many ways. He was a mysterious, private man. He was a scary man too, when he drank, and on Sundays he talked about more Pabst Blue Ribbon and football.

My day of hiking finally came to an end, and I stripped off my wet clothes as quickly as I could. My knee was swollen and throbbing, worse than before, and I took a few more Advil as I boiled rice and tried to warm my legs in my sleeping bag. I propped my leg on my pack and leaned against the wall of the shelter as I ate my bowl of rice, and it wasn't long before Saluki appeared at the shelter. He looked as wet as I felt, and he shook off the rain like a wet dog after he dropped his pack on the floor. "Man, I wish I had a blow dryer," he said, "and another one of those tacos!"

"Oh my God," I said, rolling my eyes. "I've never had a better taco in all my life!" I said, laughing. "They were super tasty."

"Damn!" he said. "They were so good."

Saluki took his time getting out of his wet clothes, and I felt lucky to be warm in my bag while he was still wet. I finished my rice dinner and granola dessert as he was just starting to cook his dinner, and I leaned out in the front of the shelter and smoked a cigarette. "Oh," he said, as he turned to me from his stove. "Did you know you were talking in your sleep?"

"Who me?" I said.

"Yeah, you. You woke me up last night. I thought you were talking to somebody outside the shelter."

"Really? I was talking in my sleep?"

"Yeah, for a while," he said.

"Huh, no kidding," I said. "What'd I say?"

"I'm not really sure, man. It was kinda jumbled and all over the place, and I was still half asleep, but you said something about engineering and not wanting to go someplace. You said you wanted to go fishing instead, but how someone wasn't around to go with you. I dunno know, man. You said something else too, but I can't remember now."

"Huh," I said. "Strange… Sorry to wake you up, man."

"No worries, Bird. Like I said, I thought you were talking to somebody outside the shelter."

Then, suddenly, it all came back to me. I had this moment of clarity where I knew enough to start putting the pieces of my day together. I had just spent a large portion of the day thinking about my father and some random dream that I couldn't remember, and then Saluki came along and told me I was talking in my sleep about engineering and wanting to go fishing. *Bam!* There it was. I took out my journal and started writing. Without even knowing it, Saluki was the go-between that connected all the unknown parts of my day to the known, and for some reason, I felt like I was having some dream-like conversation with my dead father. All day long, I couldn't remember what that dream was about, but once Saluki said what he said, I could feel this strange presence within—like some weird vibration—like I was having some long-distance-phone-call type conversation with my father. Crazy.

I kept writing. Yes, my father was an engineer, and some of the only positive memories I have of that man are when he would take me fishing at the pond near our house. I kept writing. I used to love fishing with him when I was a kid, but there were more times than not when he wouldn't show up to take me, and I'd be pissed at him for blowing me off. I reached the point of not knowing what else to write, so I put my pen down and rubbed my eyes. Saluki said something about how fast I was writing. He was writing in his journal by that time too, and then he asked me what I was writing about. I opened my mouth to tell him, but then stopped myself and lied, telling him I was writing a letter to my girl.

"Ah, you're missing your lady," he said. "Yeah, me too."

I opted not to say anything to Saluki about my father, and I pretended to go back to my writing. I scribbled a few lines here and there, but in reality, I was deep in thought about my father and what that dream might have meant. I'm not sure why I didn't share any of that with Saluki, and after a few moments of silence, he went back to his writing, and so did I.

I love the forest, but I hate the forest at the same time. I admire and respect how complex and beautiful the woods are, but I hate the fact that there is nothing else out there to distract me from my thoughts. I know that some of my questions will never be answered, but the endless woods along the trail gave my mind all the freedom it wanted to visit and re-visit and try and figure out every little thing. Yes, my father was an engineer, but he died, and that conversation about what it was like for him to be an engineer never happened. Nope, he never opened up to us at the dinner table, telling us about all the tools he worked with, or the people he worked with, and a part of me felt hollow and empty on the inside because he was gone, dead, and so were all the stories of who he was as a man. Yet, I still thought about it. I still tried to figure it all out… Was it him I was trying to figure out, or was it me?

Saluki had no idea what he had done to me. Where would I even begin if I did start talking to him about my father? I gave up. I was tired. Then the rain started to taper off, and so did I, with the night.

I went through a phase after our father left where I blamed my mother for kicking him out of the house. Andy said he was happy to see our father go, but I wasn't happy about it at all. I didn't want our family to split up, and I guess I was still too young to understand why he had to go.

Our mother struggled with two jobs to put food on the table and clothes on our backs, and rather than blaming my father for not being around to help out, I quietly blamed my mother for thinking our lives would be better off without him.

Andy liked the freedom that came along with having a single-parent household, but I didn't like the empty place at the dinner table where our father used to sit. Our house didn't seem like much of a home after dad left; it was more of a struggle to get by.

10

The Smoky Mountain range ended in a little place called Davenport Gap. A few southbound hikers had left messages in the logbooks saying that Mountain Momma's general store was a 'must see', so when the trail reached the intersecting asphalt road, I turned left and hiked the two miles into town. I didn't really need any supplies, but who wouldn't want to check out a *must see*? I had to see what all the fuss was about. And who knows, maybe Mountain Momma was one of the Hiking Mommas I had met at Rodger's place years earlier? What a trip that would be! I had to see.

And it's funny too, because when I think of what a *town* is, I naturally think of houses and grocery stores and libraries and police stations and public schools and gas stations, but when I got to Davenport Gap, I busted out laughing because the town consisted of one building, and that was Mountain Mamma's. Mountain Momma's *was* Davenport Gap!

I couldn't help but laugh when I walked through the front door of that place. I had to stop for a few seconds to take in everything I was seeing. Momma wasn't around when I got there, but I immediately gave her a ton of credit because that one building had a bunkhouse, a grocery store section, a gas pump, hot showers, a shuttle service, a post office, a cafeteria-style restaurant, a laundromat, and the most beautiful wall chalk-full of tobacco products. Momma had an entire wall packed with snuff and chew and dip and pipe tobacco and vape juices and nicotine gum and hundreds upon hundreds of cartons of cigarettes, all stacked up on one another… And man, I loved that wall! Momma must've known Tritt's!

It took me all of ten seconds to decide to stay the night at Momma's, and I rented a twenty-dollar bunk from a lady behind the counter, which was located in a rusted-out trailer on wooden blocks in the yard out back. It was the kind of trailer you hitch to the back of a truck, but there was no truck, and the trailer was missing the wheels and the axle. Momma must've had somebody build a wooden frame for the trailer to rest on, and when I walked into that trailer-bunkhouse through the back door, there were two skinny beds, one on the left side and one on the right side. I took the one on the left because it was closer to the nearby river, and I was hopeful that I'd be able to hear that river at night when I was trying to fall asleep. I was also hopeful that I'd have the trailer all to myself, but it was still pretty early in the day, and the chances were slim that another hiker wouldn't come along.

I ordered two cheeseburgers from the same counter lady who rented me the bunk, and then I took a seat in a window booth that faced the front yard. There was an old, fat man outside the window who was trying to fix a washer and dryer in the tall grass of the yard. So strange. He wore a flannel shirt and skinny blue jeans, and I laughed every time he bent over because the crack of his ass peeked out through the top of those tight jeans. He was wearing suspenders too, but they were more for show than support because they didn't do the trick too well. He had a mouthful of chew, and every couple of minutes he'd lean to the side and spit in the grass as he hoisted his pants back up. Momma must've been in the home appliance business too, because there were washers and dryers and dishwashers and stoves littered all over the yard. The old, fat guy with too much chew in his mouth must've been her handyman because he would go back and forth from one appliance to another, taking parts from one and installing them into the other. So strange. I assumed he was the same guy that built the wooden frame for the trailer I was sleeping in. He was a pretty handy guy though, and I wondered if he and Momma were hitched.

Several hikers sat around me in other booths and tables. I already knew some of them, but many were strangers to me. I was pretty happy when I saw other patrons and employees smoking inside Momma's place, so I smoked in my booth right along with them as I waited on my cheeseburgers. A few of the hikers I didn't know looked at me funny as I exhaled my cloud of smoke, but I didn't care. If Momma was gonna let me smoke inside her place, then I was damn-well gonna oblige her.

The southern slang of the older waitress who dropped off my cheeseburgers was heavier than my northern slang, and she looked weathered and worn and beat down, just like Momma's place. But she smiled big and wide, and when she asked if there was anything else I needed, I smiled back, saying I couldn't have been happier. Hell, that whole general store looked weathered and beaten down just like the waitress did, so the waitress fit in just fine at Momma's. She was the perfect waitress for that kind of place. And those burgers looked so good sitting in front of me! So, I took my time to add the pickles and the onion and the lettuce and the tomato. The buns were soft and slightly grilled as I smeared mayo on one side and mustard on the other. I couldn't wait to inhale those burgers.

I looked around the place as I ate, and I saw the cobwebs on the ceiling above and the dirt-stained baseboards on the floor below. The windows had a film on them from not being washed for God only knows how long, and the white interior walls around me had taken on a golden hue because of all the smoking. *What a place!*

In addition to the washers and dryers littered throughout the front yard, there were two big, abandoned school buses that didn't have tires. The buses were completely rusted out, and tall grass grew up alongside them, but Momma and her handyman had converted them into bunkhouses too. The big green leather seats that were once inside the buses were now scattered throughout the yard as benches for sitting, and the old handyman with his crack showing must've built the wooden bunks inside the school buses too. *What a place!*

Everybody who worked at Momma's seemed to know everyone that came in. Some people came to mail letters, while others came to buy batteries or milk or cigarettes, but every person who came in said hello to me in my booth and had a conversation with the person behind the counter. At some point, right as I was finishing up my first burger, an old lady came out of the back room of the store, and I wondered if it was Momma herself. I didn't recognize her from Roger's place, and she had a huge head of strawberry-blonde-white hair all done up in curlers, and she was smoking one of those extra-long Virginia Slim type cigarettes. The bright red lipstick she wore was smeared all over the filter of the cigarette she held, and she was humming some tune to herself as she danced around the place.

I turned my attention back to my second cheeseburger, and it wasn't long before it was gone and I was licking the juicy remains from my fingers. I lit another cigarette after my fingers dried, and I turned my attention back to the dancing woman, who was now writing something on a blackboard behind the counter. I couldn't see what she was writing, but when she finished, she cleared her throat and turned to face the seven or eight people in the place. In a real big voice, she read what she had written on the board. "The greatest love story of all time can be found in the Bible!"

And that was it. The strawberry-blonde-white-haired lady with curlers didn't say anything else, but she stood there behind the counter for several more minutes as she smiled and smoked and exhaled her cloud up toward the ceiling. *Man, what a place! What a town!*

And for all I knew, maybe that woman did understand love. Maybe she did know something about it. Hell, all I knew was that my belly was full, and I *was* in love… in love with the cigarette I was smoking and the booth I was sitting in. I propped my feet up on the other side of the booth and I smoked my smoke with a smile on my face, as if I knew something about true love too. I didn't feel like I needed to read the Bible at that moment, but I sure as hell enjoyed reading the faces of all the people that came and went from Momma's place that day. I spent the rest of the afternoon taking full advantage of the two-dollar bottomless cup of coffee Momma offered, but then, sometime later, after the sun had gone down, I decided to head off to bed in the rusted-out trailer out back.

To my surprise, I spent the night in that trailer by myself, and I woke up the next morning thinking about love and pancakes. I had seen on the menu board that Momma served pancakes for breakfast, so I hurried to get dressed and to place my order for a double stack. The thought of extra maple syrup and fluffy pancakes and sausage and coffee had my mouth watering, and I quickly smoked a cigarette as I waited.

I knew I would call Jada before I left Davenport Gap, and I sat in the same booth as the day before, thinking about what I would say to her. If I told her I was having a good time, she might be upset because I was enjoying myself without her. And if I told her I was lonely and missing her, she'd tell me to leave the trail and come home. I wasn't sure what I was going to say, but I knew I'd call her before I left Momma's place.

It was still early when I called her, and she answered the phone with that scratchy, still half-asleep tone in her voice. She said she hadn't felt well, and part of me was happy she said that, because then the conversation could be about her not feeling well instead of me not being there. She told me about the two days she took off from work and how the cough syrup she bought gave her an upset stomach and made her feel dizzy. She talked about finding a long black hair in the chicken soup she bought at the grocery store and how her nose wouldn't stop running. It was a sad conversation, to be honest, and I didn't feel like it was the right time to tell her about Momma's place and how funky and cool it was. So I lied, saying that somebody was waiting in line behind me to use the phone and that I had to go. I told her that I'd call her the next time I got the chance, and in that depressive, wispy voice of hers, she told me that she loved me.

"Me too," I replied.

My pancakes were tasty, but they had a rubbery texture and were burned along the edges. The coffee wasn't as strong and full-bodied as it was the day before, and the sausage came in patties, not links, like I wanted. The slang from my southern waitress was still thick though, and her smile was still big and wide. I knew I had a long day of hiking in front of me, and I'm glad I noticed the bright-eyed smile of my waitress, because otherwise, I knew I'd be leaving Momma's place with a bad taste in my mouth. I gave her an extra tip for the below-average pancakes, and she told me to have a great day when I bought a carton of Marlboro Reds from the wall.

Walking away from Momma's place felt ominous in a way, and I couldn't put my finger on why. The trail had me walking alongside the Pigeon River for a while, which was beautiful, yet the feeling I had was that the day would end up being long and harsh and draining. I wondered why the coffee wasn't as good that morning. I wondered why I lied to Jada when I didn't have to. I envied that southern waitress in a way, but I thanked the subtle sounds of the Pigeon River that I wasn't stuck in Davenport Gap like she appeared to be. Her life seemed hard, and I had a feeling that I was seeing the best of her.

My guidebook said I was entering the Snowbird Mountains, and the most recent logbooks I'd seen in shelters said that seventeen different hikers were within a day or two of me. I recalled how my first day on the trail said that I would have a chance to create a *fellowship with the wilderness*, and I pondered the strange sense of community I was starting to feel with the hikers and the people I had met in the forest. I looked forward to meeting those seventeen other hikers in front of me, but I still didn't like the way I felt leaving Momma's.

Dallas and Commando were two of the hikers I'd yet to meet, and suddenly, there they were. One minute I was hiking along all by myself, and the next minute, there they were, taking a break at a vista point along the trail. They were both in their mid-to-late thirties, and they were hiking together. What I noticed at once was that they were both very clean—they didn't have the rugged, rundown, exhausted look that most thru-hikers had. They wore flashy clothes that were stylish and washed. They wore brightly colored headbands and wristbands in orange and yellow. They were both freshly shaved, and they even looked like they had new haircuts. They looked like twins in how they dressed, but it only took one look to see they weren't brothers. My first impression was that they were cocky and a little full of themselves. But who knows? Maybe they thought the same of me. Our conversation was short, and I saw no good reason to find out more about them. I would either see them again or I wouldn't; I didn't really care either way.

Mariner, on the other hand, was enjoying a snack of dried apricots and figs on a tree stump when I caught up to him. He was the hiker I looked forward to meeting the most because of the silly little poems he had been leaving in the shelter logbooks. I knew I had been gaining ground on him, and from one silly poet to another, I looked forward to the conversation he and I would have.

He hardly resembled the image I had conjured of him in my head though, and I thought it was interesting that he was reading a thick, hard-covered book as he sat on the stump. With the name Mariner, I envisioned him looking like an older sea captain with weathered skin, wild hair, chapped hands, and a salt-in-pepper beard. I imagined a chiseled face with sharp features—a full, strong body. However, the Mariner I met sitting on the tree stump that day was nothing like that. This Mariner said he was from Seattle; hence, the name, and he was a little older than me, and bald. He was fifty or so pounds overweight, and there was a boyish pudginess to his cheeks and face. His hairline receded way past his forehead, and he had big ears. He looked soft and fragile and quiet—nothing like I imagined him being.

Interestingly enough, I recognized the book he was reading because it was big and blue. I had read that book several times before. I realized then that he and I might have more in common than silly little poems. The fact is that anyone who tries to live a life in sobriety is more than likely aware of the big blue book he was reading, and I smiled wide when I recognized it.

Mariner was quiet though, and I got the feeling he wasn't up for talking when I first met him. It was mid-afternoon, and there were still miles to go before the end of day, so I asked if he was hiking on to Deer Park Shelter. He said he was, so I told him I'd see him there. He nodded his head and went back to his apricots and reading.

Max Patch Road intersected the trail with a flimsy chicken-wire fence that ran along both sides of the dirt road, and as I stood there, I felt like I was on the set of one of those Jeep commercials where the newest Cherokee barreled down the road, leaving a trail of dust in its wake. The person driving the Jeep would have cool sunglasses on with a big smile, and the narrator of the commercial would say something like, "Legends aren't born; they're made." I just stood there in the middle of that dirt road for a while laughing because there was no Jeep Cherokee barreling down the road, and there was no dust ball swarming. No legends anywhere around, just me, walking alone, crossing over a dirt road into Max Patch.

Tall green grass was the only thing covering the slopes of Max Patch; there was not a tree in sight, and I felt like I was walking through the landscape of an old Wordsworth poem. That tall grass was 'fluttering and dancing in the breeze', and it tickled my fingers as I ran my open hands across the tops of those green strands. Simply mesmerizing as I made my way along the smooth trail that zigged and zagged its way forward.

At first, I wasn't sure who was hiking up in front of me, but I could see them way up ahead on the open patch. After I calculated the distance between us, I knew it would take me twenty or so minutes to catch up with them. Whoever it was had a hunched back and a slight limp to the right side, and after watching their pace for a few minutes, I figured they were only ten minutes away, not twenty. Then, twelve minutes later, I was surprised to see it was Old Smoky I was passing. "When did you pass me?" I asked, slightly embarrassed that I had been out-hiked by the old greyhound.

"Well, let's see," he said. "I probably passed you on Interstate 40 sometime late yesterday afternoon." Smoky smiled and laughed. "I caught myself a ride with a pretty young lady in a white convertible," he said, "and man, oh man, I took that ride for as long as I could!"

"You old dog," I said. "A pretty young thing picked you up smelling like you do?"

"Haha!" he howled. "She sure did! And I'll gladly give up twenty miles of hiking for a ride like that. You know what I mean, Bird?"

"Yeah, pretty young ladies are hard to come by out here," I said.

"Ain't that the truth," he replied.

I took the five-mile descent off Max Patch slowly because it was unlike anything I'd seen on the trail up to that point. Old Smoky took things even slower, and he fell further and further behind as the afternoon went along. The trail cut its way through low-lying gaps and valleys that had tiny rivers and small waterfalls that spewed out from the earth's surface. The air in those valleys kept me cool, and I crossed over manmade bridges that were constructed out of pine and oak. The valley floors were undergoing rapid changes as green life sprouted up everywhere, and young chick birds sang in nearby branches. Rust-colored squirrels scurried around, creating havoc in the winter leaves that still covered the valley floor, and the continuous howl of a red fox let me know that I was trespassing in her territory. A series of towering green pine trees that went on and on just ended in an instant, giving way to a burned section of black, naked trees, and stained tree stumps covered in sap and ash. I was overcome with the feeling that I had just walked out of a new life and into recent death. The immediate change from lush green to black death felt like Armageddon or nuclear holocaust.

I slowed my pace even more. As soon as the burned section of forest came, it left, and the life in those woods became green again. Every twist and every turn in that section of trail gave my eyes something new to admire, like the patches of wildflowers that burst up everywhere—fireworks that never left the ground. Every tree seemed to smile, and every form of life seemed to be charged with new energy. I thought about the old strawberry-blonde-white-haired lady at Mountain Momma's and how she wrote that message on the blackboard and what she said to the crowd in the store about the greatest love story of all time being in the Bible.

Well, I've never read the Bible, so I don't know much about that kind of love, but as I walked through that stretch of woods, I felt a unique kind of love for all the life surrounding me. As I hiked through those valleys and gaps and breathed that fresh air, I got a tremendous sense of timeless love from the forest and the creatures living there. It was something else.

I wasn't at Deer Park Shelter long before Mariner showed up. He was quiet again, and he went about things without using words. He changed his clothes in silence, rubbed his feet down, and started cooking beans in his pot—all without saying a word. I asked if he passed by Old

Smoky earlier on Max Patch, and he said he hadn't seen him. I chuckled at the thought of another young lady giving the old man a ride further up the trail.

Mariner and I were the only two in the shelter for a while, and after several more moments of silence, I finally asked him about the blue book he was reading. "Are you a friend of Bill W's?" I asked.

"Yep. I am now," he said.

"No kiddin'," I said. "How long you been clean for?"

"Two years," he said.

"Two years is a long time," I said.

"Yeah, it is," he said.

"I'm a friend of Bill's too," I said. "Three years for me."

"Good for you," he said.

It was like pulling teeth trying to have a conversation with Mariner, so I came right out and asked him about the poems he was writing in the logbooks.

"Those aren't my poems," he said. "My wife wrote those."

"No kidding," I said. "That's great. Where's your wife now? How come she ain't out here hiking with you?"

"She passed away a couple years ago," he said.

"Ah, man," was all I could say in response. I didn't have any other words, so I didn't say anything. I wasn't expecting that. Mariner just kept looking into his pot of beans as he stirred, and I'm not sure why, but I held my breath for a long time as I sat there watching him. I thought he might say something more, like how she died, but he didn't. Eventually I exhaled, and I told him I was sorry for his loss. "I lost a good friend not too long ago myself," I said. "It's tough."

"Yeah, it's tough," he said.

I felt like I was being saved when I heard the footsteps of somebody else coming up toward the shelter. Mariner continued to sit and stir in silence as I got up to see who else would be joining us in the shelter that night. "Well, hello there, young man," said Old Smoky, as he turned the corner and came into sight. "Nice to see you again, Bird."

"Same here, Smoky. Same here."

"Sure was pretty hiking those last few miles, wasn't it?"

"Sure was," I said. "But was it as pretty as the little lady in the white convertible?"

"I wouldn't go that far!" he said, laughing.

Smoky poked his head inside the shelter and said hello to Mariner. I asked Smoky if he had met Mariner already, and he said he met him earlier in the day on Max Patch. Mariner didn't look up or say anything as he tasted his beans, and I decided not to say anything either. I didn't see the point in it.

It was quiet in the shelter that night, and I woke up early the next morning before the two of them. I felt bad for Mariner as I drank my morning coffee and got ready for the day out near the fire pit. I wondered if he and his wife had plans to hike the trail together, but she died before that happened. Maybe leaving her poems in the shelters was proof that she was there with him. I made sure to sign the logbook before I left, and I wondered if Mariner would leave another one of his wife's poems behind. I figured he would.

It was a short three-mile hike that morning into the town of Hot Springs, and I was looking forward to seeing the sights and stocking up on some supplies. I had plenty of smokes, but I was craving cheese and sugar and roast beef. I craved bread and cake and butter and bacon, so I was excited to see what Hot Springs had to offer.

I liked how the trail cut right down the middle of Main Street in Hot Springs. I never had to leave the trail because Main Street *was* the trail, and I thought that was pretty cool. It was a cute little town, and it was nothing like Davenport Gap because it had restaurants and hotels and side-street houses with residents out walking their dogs. It had paved roads, police cars, and blue mailboxes on street corners.

It was still early in the day when I got to Hot Springs, so there was a mid-afternoon busyness to the town. People came and went from the hardware store and the corner cafe. Cars stopped at the center of town crosswalk and waited for pedestrians to make their way across the street—everyone waved and smiled and took their time. Then I saw the post office and the outfitter store right next to it, and there were hikers by the dozen around that place. Some of them I knew, but most of them I didn't.

I felt excited walking toward them. I saw Dallas and Commando sitting on a bench, still color-coordinated, and I assumed they hitched a ride to town like old Smoky, because there was no way they had passed me since I saw them last. Shenandoah was there, and so were Gingerbread Man and Afterburner. Violet and Blue were there, and so were Tortoise and Hare. Jellybean, Tucker, and Crazy Legs Lance were there as well, and they were all hikers I'd yet to meet. I walked toward them, then up to them, with my hand outstretched to meet them all.

11:03pm

Our father sobered up for a couple of years when we were in grade school, and those were the years our family went on vacations to Niagara Falls and North Carolina. The place we went to in Carolina was rundown, a lot like Davenport Gap, but it was near a lake, and we fished, swam, and ate hot dogs by the fire.

"He'll drink again," said my brother about our father. "He won't stay this way for long." And he was right. It wasn't long before dad was coming home all lit up again.

Mother took us to a therapist after dad moved out, and we rolled our eyes and sat there with our arms crossed over our chests. We were handed pillows shaped like baseball bats, and the shrink told us to take out our aggressions on one another. My brother and I teamed up on our sister, backing her into a corner, and she screamed bloody hell until our mother stepped in to help her. Later that night, mother questioned just how effective pillow-fight therapy was.

11

Violet and Blue were Italian sisters from California, and they wanted to hike the trail before they went off to college. They were eighteen and nineteen. Blue was on the quiet side and hadn't shaved her legs or pits since she left home, and Violet constantly hummed a tune to herself while she wrote in her journal. They hiked together, and better yet, they shared the things they carried. Violet carried the tent and sleeping bags, while Blue carried the food and clothes— they liked how their packs were only twenty pounds each instead of thirty-five or forty. With a shrug and a smile, Blue finally said, "If you can still smell yourself, then you ain't been out here long enough!" And that was the truth, because I could smell Blue's body stench from five feet away. It must have been weeks since she showered. Violet, on the other hand, was more feminine, and she carried disposable wipes that she used to clean her lady parts.

Shenandoah was a red-headed guy around fifty years old. He was fit and tall with a few jailhouse arm tattoos, and the way he talked made me think he missed being in his twenties. He had a loud voice and a huge laugh, and everybody could tell he had a thing for Violet. He would tell stories loud enough for everyone to hear them, but his eyes were constantly glued on her. It was like his stories were just for her ears. Violet seemed to enjoy the flattery, but it was apparent that Shenandoah was fishing in the dark.

Tortoise and Hare were a sight to see because Hare was a really big woman and Tortoise was a petite little thing. They were family, an aunt and niece, and they hiked together as well. Apparently, Hare's husband passed away unexpectedly, but his dream was to one day hike the Appalachian Trail. He never realized that dream, so Hare thought she'd do it for him. As a bigger woman in her late-forties, Hare was afraid to hike the trail alone, so Tortoise agreed to join her. They laughed a lot and told little inside jokes that only the two of them understood. Hare talked about losing weight, while Tortoise talked about gaining weight, but they both talked about their cravings for pork and potato chips.

Afterburner and Gingerbread Man were both very athletic, and they met each other online before they started hiking. From what I could gather, they met in some online chatroom where the focus was on high endurance, long distance, speed hiking. They met, became friends, then they agreed to hike the trail together—a buddy-system of sorts, and they were hiking or jogging anywhere from twenty-five to thirty-five miles a day. They wore running sneakers instead of boots, and they carried as little as possible, just enough food for a day or two. They wanted to complete the whole trail in under three months, but they were held up in Hot Springs for a couple days because Afterburner twisted an ankle and opted to rest up and ice himself down in Hot Springs. I wasn't sure when they passed me on the trail, but I was certain that I wouldn't see them again after they left

Hot Springs. Hiking thirty-plus miles a day seemed like insanity to me.

Jellybean and Crazy Legs Lance were washing their clothes at the local laundromat when I met them, and they talked non-stop about Nascar and drag racing. It was nice to meet them, but they wouldn't shut up about two things I knew nothing about. I never saw the point of driving in circles at high speeds, but the two of them couldn't get enough of it.

Then there was Tucker, who was eating a peanut butter and banana sandwich by herself on a picnic table. She was alone, but she didn't look uncomfortable being alone. Tucker had beautiful blue eyes and a confidence about herself that made my stomach twitch. Perhaps I was missing Jada when I first met Tucker, but man, she was beautiful. Her straight brown hair and the faint freckles along the bridge of her nose... man, I had to look away because I knew I'd get caught up in staring.

Then, I felt hungry and horny, so I turned my attention to eating roast beef and cheese and bread and smelling my clean clothes from the dryer. And I needed to find a place to sleep that night... without Tucker. Perhaps I'd see and talk to Tucker again; I sure wanted to, but there was another part of me that hoped I didn't.

Old Smoky showed up in Hot Springs later that afternoon, and he was looking for someone to split a hotel room with him. He had heard that Ramsey's hardware store had an apartment for rent above the store and that it was only fifty-five bucks for the night. I didn't want to spend that kind of money on a place to sleep, but the thought of a hot shower and a warm bed took over, and I agreed.

After sleeping for ten hours, I woke up feeling fresh. It was late in the morning, and I brewed some coffee and ate the leftovers of my roast beef sandwich before taking another shower. My legs felt strong and muscular, and my knee wasn't swollen or throbbing. It felt pretty sweet to slide into clean clothes that smelled like flowers.

I could hear the customers coming and going from the hardware store below, and I walked out onto the little balcony of the apartment to see Violet sitting on a bench in front of the store. She was humming a tune to herself and writing in her journal. I walked downstairs with my coffee and took a seat next to her on the bench. "What are you writing?" I asked.

"Oh, you know, song lyrics, and some other stories about being on the trail."

"You write songs?" I asked.

"Yeah. I'd like to get a band together one day, maybe while I'm away at school. Who knows, maybe I can cut an album or something cool like that."

"Sounds like a plan," I said. "You're gonna be the lead singer, right?"

"Yeah, I love singing," she said.

"Well, let me hear something," I said.

"What… Right here? Right now?"

"Hell, yeah," I said. "You just start singing a song, and once I get in rhythm with you, I'll start drumming on the bench here. We can start our own little band right here," I said.

She laughed. "I dunno. We're sitting in front of a hardware store!"

"Who cares?" I said. "Come on, it'll be great."

I was kinda surprised when Violet agreed to sing, but she did. She closed her journal and then closed her eyes. Her somewhat embarrassed half-smile faded away quickly as she straightened her spine and cleared her throat. I took a sip from my coffee as she readjusted herself on the bench. She started to hum a beat, and then she started swaying her head back and forth—I could tell she was trying to align her body to the words she would sing. Then she opened her mouth and started singing. The words were soft and light at first, but they grew in energy and volume as she built momentum. She started to move her arms and hands in a way that really plugged her in. Her eyes remained closed, but then she stood up and really started to sing.

At first, I was listening to her humming beat so I could maybe join in with my bench drums, but I quickly lost track of that because her voice simply took my breath away. The weight of her words seemed to rest on my shoulders, and the gravity of her song had me motionless in my seat on the bench. People walking along the street turned their heads to see this hiker girl singing. People leaving the hardware store stopped and listened before getting back into their cars. Violet was so lost in the moment that she seemed elevated, like she was walking on a cloud all by herself. Her arms and hands continued to add movement to the song she sang, and her words created this melody that seemed to soothe everyone in earshot. Remarkable.

Then it was over, and Violet opened her eyes. The half-embarrassed smile came back to her face as she covered her mouth with both hands, surprised that she actually sang a song on a Hot Spring's street corner. I couldn't help but applaud, shout, and hug her. "That was something else!" I said. "Amazing! Where the hell did you get a voice like that?"

Violet laughed. "My momma," she said. "My momma is a beautiful singer."

"Wow!" I said. "That was incredible."

"Bravo!" we heard from behind us. "Magnificent!" shouted Old Smoky from the balcony above the hardware store. "That was one helluva way for me to start my day, and I thank you, Miss Violet, for the beautiful song."

"You're welcome," replied Violet, as she took a long bow before her audience and continued to laugh.

I didn't want to leave Hot Springs, but I felt like I needed to. If I stayed, I'd spend more money, and I didn't want to drain my limited funds. I had already spent more than I planned. I had a blast in Hot Springs, but it was time for me to push on. Several hikers had already left earlier that morning, and I knew I was getting a late start to the hiking day, so I bid farewell to Hot Springs around noon, and mapped out the ten-mile hike to get me to Spring Mountain Shelter. I was hoping to get there by nightfall.

I could feel my mood changing as I left Hot Springs behind. The trail had me climbing up and up for some four miles, and I could feel that depressive state of mind come over me as I trudged on. The sky promised rain sometime soon, and I didn't want that. I didn't want my fresh, clean clothes to get sweaty, stinky, and wet. Not yet.

After an hour or so, I could see the town of Hot Springs below me to the south, some fifteen hundred feet down, and I wanted to be back there singing songs on hardware store benches and flipping through cable TV channels as I fell asleep. I wanted to be clean and dry and fat on roast beef sandwiches and potato salad. I wanted to flop more on that living room couch and take showers that were too hot. I wanted soft sheets for sleeping and a street-side view from a small balcony.

Then I heard it. *Bloop.* I heard one, then another. I stopped. I waited. Then I heard it again, *bloop*. I was hiking past Lover's Leap Rock when I came across a small pond that had decent-sized fish jumping. First, I heard it, but then I saw it. Every jump had a splash that sent ripples across the surface, and I wished I had my fishing pole and some fat earthworms.

I took off my pack and walked around the edges of the little pond. I saw groups of baby minnows and tadpoles swimming along the shoreline. I saw tiny bubbles rising to the surface from somewhere below, and I wanted to see another jump. I took a seat in the shade of an old oak tree, and I thought about how I loved fishing in ponds as a kid. I rested my head on the hard bark surface of the tree, as I focused in on the water's surface. I waited and I watched, and I chuckled at myself because, as a kid, I would wait and watch just like that, and as soon as the jump came, I would cast my line right to that exact spot. So, I waited, and I watched, and when that jump happened, I threw my imaginary line right there. I could picture it all so clearly. Too bad I left my fishing pole behind in that Georgia cabin. *Bloop.*

The Rex Pulford Memorial came out of nowhere, and it stopped me dead in my tracks. I was getting close to Spring Mountain Shelter and the sun was nearly set, but then I saw it right there in front of me, and I stopped. It was a stone memorial dedicated to a 1983 thru-hiker named Rex

Pulford. Apparently, he dropped dead of a heart attack in the exact spot I was standing. And it was strange, because I started feeling this weird vibration running through me as I stood there—I chalked it up to coincidence rather than Rex himself paying me a visit.

I looked around at the landscape, and I thought about what it would be like to die right there. And honestly, it wouldn't have been so bad. It was beautiful and quiet, and the birds were chirping in the nearby trees. I mean, who wouldn't want to die in a place like that? But then I thought about Rex never making it all the way to Maine, and I felt bad for him because that was his plan, right? I mean, he never made it there, and that's obviously what he wanted.

I thought about old Rex for a while longer as I kept hiking. I asked myself if his time on the trail was a half-empty or a half-full story? I wasn't sure. I mean, his plan to hike the whole trail, right? And he was taking the steps to get to Maine, right? But he didn't make it. He never got there. I thought about that some more. I didn't know if I should feel happy or sad for Rex. I felt a need to pick a side...

Who cares if he didn't make it all the way! Big deal, I thought. At least he was taking the steps to get there. I started to admire Rex's story—definitely a half-full story. But then I started wondering if Rex was aware that he never made it to Maine. Does he even know that he never got there? And if he does know, does that mean he's sitting up there in Heaven feeling all pissed-off that he didn't make it? *Oh boy,* I thought. Now I'd really done it. I opened up that can of worms that deals with the afterlife—*and wow*—I could think about that for hours and hours. Who knows if Rex knows? Maybe he did make it up to Maine?

I spent the night in Spring Mountain Shelter by myself, and I was surprised by that. I figured there would be at least a few hikers from Hot Springs that would stop there, but that wasn't the case. And it was strange too, because on the nights when there were other people in the shelters, I wanted to be alone, but on nights when I was alone, I wanted the company of other hikers. Strange. I had a lot of fun in Hot Springs meeting those other hikers, and I guess I was craving a little more of that.

I sat by the fire for a while that night as I replayed Violet's song in my mind a few times and how she put both hands over her mouth in embarrassment when she was done singing. I loved how Old Smoky thanked her from the balcony without a shirt on. He sure was a cool old man! I ate extra chicken and rice as I thought more about Hot Springs, and I smoked a few extra cigarettes while I warmed my feet by the fire.

I never spent much time thinking about God as a kid. I had a hard time believing that some guy named Jesus died on a cross and then came back to life a few days later. It was hard for me to believe that somebody like that could part the sea or feed the masses with only a couple of fish and a piece of stale bread. I mean, those stories sounded more like fairy tales, and once I found out the bad news that Santa Claus wasn't a real guy, I sorta dismissed God or Jesus the same way I dismissed Santa. And as I grew a little older and came to understand the impossibility of Santa Claus going around to every single house in the world, I wondered why other people didn't think the same thing about God or Jesus. I mean, it was all impossible, right? It just simply couldn't happen, right?

Then something happened to me the morning after I left Spring Mountain Shelter, and I've had a really hard time explaining it to myself in a way that makes much sense. I guess I never really believed in coincidence all that much either, the same way I didn't believe in Jesus or Santa when I got older, but on the morning after I saw the Rex Pulford Memorial, I came across something on the trail that simply had my mind spinning. It blew me away.

I was hiking along the trail around nine or ten in the morning, and I saw something in the middle of the trail up ahead. As I got closer, I could see that it was thirty or forty butterflies, and they were all in a pack on the ground. They weren't flying around or anything like that, they were all on the ground, and they were all hunched together too, in some tight-knit group. They were all really still. Then I saw how there were several different species of butterflies in the group—monarch butterflies, painted lady butterflies, blue butterflies, and others that had real fancy patterns on their wings. It was beautiful and pretty incredible to see. I slowly took off my pack, and I kneeled down in front of them. It was amazing how they let me get so close to them—I could have reached out and touched them if I wanted to. Not one of them flew away.

I noticed how, in the middle of the pack, there was a dead butterfly. It was just lying there, belly up, completely dead. Then, to my disbelief, I saw one butterfly in the group inch its way up to the dead one and touch it all over—body, wings, and head. And after that one finished touching the dead one, it backed away and let the next one step forward.

And the next one did the exact same thing. It touched the dead butterfly all over and then backed away. This went on for several minutes as each butterfly paid their respects to the dead one. And I just couldn't believe how orderly these different species of butterflies were with one another—I couldn't believe the compassion and intellect. I mean, holy shit! They weren't pushing each other out of the way or flying around to distract the little ceremony that was happening—these butterflies were having a friggin' funeral for their dead friend, and I just couldn't believe it! They were totally respectful of the moment, like they knew exactly what was going on. Amazing! I must have laid on the trail for a good ten minutes as each butterfly went up to the fallen one.

And it's moments like that that made me wish I'd brought my friggin' phone with me. *But no, not me!* I wanted to hike the trail without my phone—you know, old-school—because if I was going to document anything while hiking, it would be through writing in my journal, not through pictures or videos or Instagram posts. And it pissed me off too, because a video of that butterfly funeral would have been pretty sweet.

I sat up after the funeral ended, and I tried to write out the words that would fit with what I'd just seen. I couldn't do it. So, I smoked a cigarette and watched as the different butterflies dispersed from the group and took flight again. I put my journal away with the hope that the right words would eventually come to me.

My pack was still heavy, and my legs were still sore, but after seeing those butterflies do their thing, I felt like some big door in the sky had opened up a little bit for me to see through. The impossible was still impossible, but maybe not as much as I thought. I mean, a man still couldn't come back to life after being dead for three days, but before that morning happened, butterflies couldn't host funerals either. So, it was like this door to certain possibilities was opening up for me, and I hiked along that day feeling light and open to certain possibilities.

Somehow, a *fellowship with the wilderness* was no longer some bullshit slogan carved into a rock by some outdoor enthusiasts looking to entice people like me onto the trail. I don't know if that butterfly funeral made me feel more bonded to the forest or the creatures that live in it, but I certainly felt like the wilderness or God or Jesus or Santa Claus or Rex Pulford were trying to teach me something about life and death and nature and the cycle of it all. Fascinating.

The sky was bound to cry that day, and it did, around noon. I could see the rain coming, so I took out the trash bag I stole from the hardware store apartment, and I did my best to cover up my pack. It was awful when my pack got wet because, even though it was water-resistant, it still got saturated and heavier. I'm not sure how, but everything inside the pack would get damp and wet too, even with the plastic lining on the inside. I guess I'm not sure what water-resistant really means, but I was happy to have that trash bag, that's for sure. Obviously, the heavier the rain, the more wet things got, so I took my time and made sure that that trash bag covered the whole pack.

But the rain came hard, really hard, and it felt like I was being shot in the face with little bee-bee gun pellets. The winds picked up too, and that made my protective trash bag cover flap and flutter and eventually pull away from my pack. I started cursing and ranting about the rain and the bullshit wetness that would surely soak everything in my pack and, *"What the fuck!"* I shouted at the top of my lungs…

And, of course, that's when I saw her, some twenty feet up in front of me, at the bend in the trail, sheltering herself under some thick pine trees. And I felt so foolish as I approached her with my flapping trash bag shield that wasn't working, and my waterlogged boots, and my verbal rants about the rain. Without question, she heard me screaming bloody hell at the rain, so I tried to play it cool as I walked up to her saying, "Hey, Tucker. How's it going?"

"Hello, Bird," she said with a laugh. "You're looking pretty wet there. Everything okay?"

I just started laughing because there really wasn't anything else I could say or do. I knew I looked pretty foolish with a torn trash bag hanging off my pack, and I knew she heard me swearing the rain up and down, so I just laughed. "Could you do me a favor?" I eventually said. "Could you please take this trash bag off my pack?"

"Haha," she laughed. "Sure, I can do that for you."

After she took the trash bag off and I tucked it away, I found myself looking into those eyes of hers. Man, they were pretty! But I knew she heard me losing my mind over the rain, so I didn't feel like that was the right time to strike up a smooth conversation with her. I felt way too foolish for that. "I'm already soaked," I said. "I'm just gonna keep on going until I stop for the day. You gonna stay here until the rain stops?" I asked.

"Yeah, I'm not all that wet," she said, "so I'm gonna wait it out here."

"Okay. I'll see you up the trail then."

"You bet," she said.

"Thanks for helping me with the trash bag," I said.

"My pleasure," she smirked.

I felt wet and embarrassed as I hiked along. I was all up in my head as I thought about how stupid I must have looked to her and how ridiculous I must have sounded. I was grateful I didn't try to shrug the whole thing off like I wasn't pissed off or anything like that though. If I wasn't one hundred percent sure she heard me cursing like that, then I might have tried to play it cooler, like a little rain was good for the soul, or some bullshit like that, but I knew she heard me, and I'm just glad I decided to laugh it off instead. What a day! What a fucking day!

I arrived at Little Laurel Shelter earlier than I thought I would, but I was waterlogged, and spent, and done for the day. I felt like a drowned rat, and it felt pretty shitty to pull off my wet clothes only to replace them with damp ones. Everything in nature was soaked that day, so there wasn't going to be a fire in the pit where I could dry my clothes. I set up a makeshift clothesline in the shelter instead and hung up everything I had. I slid into my damp sleeping bag, and once the chill was gone, I brewed some coffee and made my dinner. The rain eventually tapered off, but the clouds remained misty and moist. The hot coffee and rice and beans warmed me from the inside out.

Tucker showed up at Little Laurel a couple hours after I got there, and she didn't waste any time getting out of her wet clothes and into dry ones. We were the only two in the shelter, and I was surprised at how easy it was for her to change clothes in front of me, and then to pick the toe jam from her feet. And after she ate dinner, she didn't even think twice about grabbing her toilet paper and saying, "Nature calls."

Tucker wasn't only beautiful, but she had this confidence as she went about things. And it baffled me that she could so easily strip, almost naked, in front of a stranger like me and then trim her toenails in front of me. I mean, I don't know about anyone else, but I get embarrassed when I grab the toilet paper in front of a beautiful woman that I don't know. And I think twice about picking my nose and feet in front of people I don't know. And I certainly don't burp or fart! But she did all those things with ease and grace. She was something else.

Tucker told me about the town she came from in Pennsylvania and how she was considering the National Guard after the trail. She talked about wanting to see the world and trying to learn something from the different cultures that were out there.

"Why the trail?" I asked. "What brought you out here?"

"I dunno," she said. "I feel like life is gonna get pretty busy with kids and careers and whatnot, so I wanted to cut loose and do something like this before things got too busy for me."

"You're telling my story now," I said. "I need some adventure in my life before I don't have time for it anymore."

"Yeah," she said. "We're all gonna get sucked up pretty soon with pursuing that *American Dream* thing, and I want to make sure I live a little bit before I go throwing thirty-plus years of life into kids and white picket fences and two cars in the garage."

"I couldn't agree more," I said.

We talked some more about the so-called *American Dream*, and then I told her about the butterfly funeral I saw earlier in the day. Tucker leaned in to hear more about that, and I milked every second of that story with her, embellishing certain parts as I went along, because I liked the way she looked at me when I spoke. There were sixty butterflies instead of thirty or forty in the story I told her, and I even touched a few of them in the version she heard. Then I told her about how I buried the little dead butterfly, which, of course, I never did. Man, she was pretty! And I liked the way she looked at me.

Tucker pulled a small, lightweight quilt from her pack, and she wrapped herself up in it. The quilt was older with frayed edges, and it had little picture patches and embroidered dates all over it. When I asked about it, she said her mother made the quilt for her when she was a girl and how she brings it everywhere with her. "Each patch and each date is a memory, and each memory has a story," she said.

I paid close attention to Tucker as she told me the stories about her quilt, because then I had the chance to look her in the eye as she spoke. And I soaked up every ounce of that, just like Old Smoky did on his white convertible ride with his young lady. But then, a few minutes after our stories were told, Tucker said goodnight and rolled over with her quilt. Just like that, it was over. *Poof.*

And there I sat. Just when I thought things were getting warmed up with Tucker, she pulled the rug out from underneath me and went to bed. There I sat, for a while longer, smile on my face, because it had been quite the day! A beautiful girl and butterflies—what a day! I pulled out my journal and started to write about all the things that happened that day. I wrote about the rain and the cursing and the life and the death I saw. I wrote about the trash bag and the beautiful eyes. What a day! I wrote about the various color patterns on the wings of those butterflies, and how it all meant something more than what I could see. What a day! I wrote about Tucker's breathing as she fell asleep.

Then I thought about Robert and how I hadn't thought of him or talked to him for a while. So, with him in mind, I wrote a letter to him about how I was spending the night beside some beautiful woman in a shelter in the woods. I knew he'd be jealous, so I poked fun at him in the letter, telling him how much he'd love Tucker. "She's something else!" I wrote. "It's been one hell of a day!"

The sunbeams through the trees woke me up the next morning when they reached my eyes. The temperature was cold and the winds were strong, but the sunbeams felt great on my face. Tucker was already awake, sitting cross-legged in some yoga pose, eating oatmeal. "Mornin'," she said.

"Morning," I said, sitting up. "Ya know, my legs would snap in half if I tried to sit like that."

Tucker laughed. "It's my way of stretching in the morning. You should try it," she said.

I opted to stretch my arms over my head as I moaned that stiff morning moan. "I don't know," I said. "I think something would fall off if I tried twisting myself up like that."

"Keeps my legs and back from cramping during the day," she said.

"Okay," I said. "I'll buy that." I started to pull together my morning coffee, but I had to pause because of a strange feeling on my head. The knitted wool hat I wore while sleeping kept my ears and forehead nice and warm, but I could feel a chilly breeze on the top of my head. It was the strangest sort of feeling, and when I took my hat off, I could see a huge hole in the knitting. "What the hell?" I said. I showed my hat to Tucker, and she immediately started laughing. "What's so funny?" I said. "My hat has a huge hole in it!"

"Looks like the mice or some rat got to your hat last night while you were sleeping." She laughed some more. "Hey, they need something warm to sleep in too, ya know."

"Man, I love this hat! What the… Hey, wait a minute," I said, reaching for the top of my head. "Am I missing any hair?"

Tucker unfolded herself from her yoga pose and leaned forward to take a look. "Maybe a couple ends were nibbled off," she said, laughing even harder.

"And what about you?" I said. "Did the rats nibble away at you last night, too?"

"Nope," she said. "I'm without any holes or missing parts this morning. They must not like the way I smell."

As I sat there with my morning coffee, I knew I had a decision to make. I could either hike along with Tucker throughout the day, milking that for everything I could, or I could leave the shelter before she did that morning. I was dying for a cigarette, and I wouldn't smoke in front of her, so I contemplated my options as I drank my coffee.

Needing a smoke won out, which I knew it would, so as Tucker finished up her morning yoga session on the shelter floor, I shouldered my pack and told her it was nice spending the night talking with her.

"You too," she said. "Maybe I'll see you later on down the trail."

"Maybe," I said. "Happy hiking, Tucker."

My smoke tasted great, and I really needed it, but once it was finished, I started thinking about the things that *might* have happened if I decided to stay with Tucker. I was glad I didn't stay and hike along with her, but I certainly enjoyed the little fantasy I played out that morning as I hiked along—the snack we'd have at the vista overlooking Blackstack Cliffs, the laughing, the storytelling, the lunch we'd share at Jerry Cabin Shelter, the affectionate smiles we'd offer up to one another, the tent we'd pitch in the woods at Devil's Fork Gap, the three days we'd spend there, naked of course, as we talked more about *our* American Dream, our other dreams, the National Guard, and the names of the six kids we'd have… I lit another cigarette and started thinking about Jada back home. What a bastard I was, thinking about Tucker like that! I needed to think more about Jada like that, who was patiently waiting for me to finish playing Huckleberry Finn in the woods. It should have been her in that fantasy tent with me at Devil's Fork Gap, not Tucker. It should have been her naked in my tent with me… I started missing Jada. What an asshole I was!

I tried to stop thinking about naked fantasies with Tucker and Jada by focusing on the wildflower clusters on the forest floor and how the wind prompted them to dance around like packs of small children in a school play—they were beautiful. I tried looking for the woven caterpillar nests in low-lying branches and thought about how it wouldn't be long before those caterpillars were free to chomp on fresh green leaves. I started looking for the colonies of ants in formation as they marched over timbered logs and carried things twice their weight, but I couldn't find them. I tried to smell the fresh minty pine scent in the air, which I knew was there, but I couldn't. The only smell coming through that afternoon was that of the Marlboro I was smoking.

I thought about Robert and the letter I wrote him. I thought about how heroin and fentanyl reminded me of the burned-black section of trail I hiked through a few days earlier. I thought of old Rex Pulford and the engraved stone marking his death spot. Does it even matter that he didn't make it to Maine? I thought of the colored butterfly patterns, and I wondered why I lied to Tucker when I told her the story of the butterfly funeral. I thought of my brother and my sister and my mother—I wondered where they fit into all of this. I could hear the chatter of the birds, some near and some far away, but I couldn't see them because I was looking down at my wet boots as I trudged along. I focused more on that—my trudging. I listened to my breathing as I watched the steps my boots took. I synchronized my breathing to the steps I walked, and I eventually found my cadence. I became numb to everything else as I breathed and stepped and breathed and stepped.

11:58pm

Andy and I used to fish a lot at the pond near our house when we were younger. He used to get a kick out of finding frogs and putting firecrackers in their mouths. He'd light the fuse and scream, "Fire in the hole!"

Andy also tried making out with my girlfriend a few times back in high school when he was wasted. Not only was my girlfriend offended by what Andy tried to do, but she eventually broke up with me because she felt uncomfortable coming over to our house. Andy never owned up to what he did, and I remember him calling her a bitch anyway. "You're better off without her," he said.

12

It was the freight train whistle right outside of Erwin, Tennessee that snapped me back into reality. I'm not sure how or why, but when I did the math in my trail book, I realized I had just hiked forty-one miles in less than thirty-six hours. From Flint Mountain Shelter to the Nolichucky River, I was like a man on a mission, but when I heard that engine whistle blow, it was like I was smacked back into reality. I looked again at my trail book, and it was like High Rock and Big Stamp and Spivey Gap and Temple Hill Gap were all blurs in my memory… I remembered being in those places, but not really. Where did my mind go the last two days? I wasn't sure. Lots of blurry trudging.

I could see the town of Erwin below me, some two thousand feet, and I could see the train as it rolled alongside the river. It was beautiful. I was sore all over. My legs hurt, and I was running low on water. I didn't feel like smoking. Even though I was grateful to hike so far in such a short period of time, I was happy for that whistle and how it pulled my head out of my ass.

As I entered the town of Erwin, I could smell brownies or cookies baking somewhere. I could hear dogs barking in backyards on Chestoa Pike, but I couldn't see them. I knew there was a hiker hostel on the street I was walking on because that's what the trail book said, and when I heard the sounds of the Cat Stevens song, *Trouble*, I walked toward the music. As I got closer, the music got louder, and I realized the hiker hostel was the source of the music. I loved that song because my mother loved that song, and I remembered the times she'd play and sing that song in the car as she drove. *"Oh, trouble set me free,"* she used to sing.

The guy who owned the hiker hostel went by the name of Uncle Johnny, and he sat on the front porch of his hostel as I walked up. He had a Budweiser in one hand and a cigarette in the other. "You like Cat Stevens?" he asked.

"Sure do," I said.

"Well, that's great," he said, "cuz it's the Cat Steven's hour round here right now."

"Sweet," I said. I shook Uncle Johnny's hand, and he welcomed me to his place. He offered me a beer, but I asked for water instead.

"Help yourself," he said. "Bottled water is in the fridge."

Johnny's place was top-notch because everything was brand new. Everything, and I mean everything, was made out of pine. Pine cabinets and walls and floors. Pine countertops and coffee tables and chairs. Pine ceilings and porches and bunks for the hikers to sleep in. The smell of pine throughout the place made me feel warm and welcome, and when I went back out onto the front porch, I sat in the pine rocking chair next to Johnny.

"Feels good to sit down, doesn't it?"

"Sure does," I said. "It's been a long couple of days."

"What's your name?" he asked.

"Bird," I said. "I go by Bird."

"And what's your real name?" he asked.

"Funny," I said. "You're the first person out here to ask me that. My name is Andrew, Andy for short."

"Nice to meet you, Andy. Where you from?"

"Boston," I said. "But it's been a while since I've been there. Been living down in Florida the last four or five years."

"You a Red Sox fan?" he asked.

"Absolutely," I said. "I love the Sox and the Pats and the B's and the C's."

"Well," said Johnny, as he started rocking in his chair, "I'm from the Bronx, and we have a rule around here that every Sox fan has to sleep in the doghouse out back."

"Haha," I laughed. "Is that made out of pine, too?"

"Sure is," he said, laughing. "No, for real though. I fuckin' hate the Red Sox!"

"Well, Johnny," I said, "I hate the Yankees probably as much as you hate the Sox, so the doghouse is fine by me."

We laughed about that for a while, but then Johnny started to ask me about the trail and what it was like for me. I lit a cigarette and told him about the wall of tobacco at Momma's place in Davenport Gap, and we both laughed as I told him about belt buckle Bob in Georgia and the southern boy at Tritt's who spit chew juice every few seconds. I told him about Jeff and Nancy at the Fontana Motel and how they were some of the nicest people I'd ever met.

"That's what I love about this trail," he said. "You meet some of the best people in the world along the way."

"I'll second that," I said.

"I hiked the trail back in 2002," he said, "and ever since then, I knew I wanted to retire somewhere along the trail."

"And that's why you have this place?" I asked.

"Yep, that's right. I left New York after my divorce about three years ago, and I came down here and bought this place. You should've seen it back then," he said, rolling his eyes. "This place was a real shit hole! It took me all of two years to do this place over."

"Why all the pine?" I asked.

"Cuz it's cheap," he said, laughing. "And cuz it reminds me of the shelters along the trail."

"Now that you mention it, this place does resemble some of the shelters."

"Yeah, I had some pictures of the shelters I took back in '02, and when I got this place, I decided to outfit it like some of the shelters."

"Very cool," I said. "And what about Erwin? Any other Yankee fans living here?"

"Ha!" he said. "There are a couple Mets fans on the other side of town, but I'm the only Yankee I know of."

"Any Sox fans?" I asked.

"Couple of'm right over there," he said, pointing across the street, laughing.

"Nice," I smirked.

Shenandoah, Naked Dog, Coke and Saluki were the other hikers staying at Uncle Johnny's that night. They arrived late in the day, so there wasn't much hanging around with those guys before we crashed and went to bed. It was great to see Saluki again though, and after we chatted for a few, we realized we were hiking within a day or so of each other for some time. "I've been right behind you for days now," he said. "Glad to finally catch up with you and see you again."

"Good to see you too, man."

Uncle Johnny was a great host, and we woke up the next morning to the smell of bacon frying, eggs snapping, and coffee brewing. He sat at the table with us as we ate, and I could tell he was in his glory with all the stories being told around his table. I hadn't met Naked Dog or Coke yet, so it was good to break bread with them and talk about the trail thus far. We all had stories to tell that morning. Shenandoah was still talking about Violet and how hard it was not to slow his pace so he could hike along with her. I nodded my head as I thought about Tucker, but I opted not to tell him or anyone else about my desire to stay and hike with her. I did tell the story of the rats eating my hat to pieces though, and I even pulled it out of my pack as proof. "Gimme that," said Uncle Johnny, as he reached for the hat. "I'll stitch this thing back up for you in no time," he said. "It'll be good as new."

"Really?" I said.

"Absolutely," he replied.

"Even though I'm a Sox fan?"

"Ha!" he smirked. "Yeah, yeah, even if you're a Sox fan. Gimme an hour or so, and I'll break out my sewing kit."

After breakfast, each of the hikers started doing their own thing. Naked Dog started reading a Dennis Lehane book in the pine bunk he slept in, Coke was on his way to the grocery store for supplies, Saluki took a nap in the front porch rocking chair, so I decided to take a walk down to the Nolichucky River. I had my journal and another cup of Uncle Johnny's coffee with me, so I took a seat along the riverbank and watched the current work its way around rocks of all sizes and tree branches that had fallen.

I hadn't called Jada yet, but I knew I would before I left Erwin. Thinking about her was easy to do as I sat by the river—the choppy little whitecaps and the flow of that water put my mind at ease, and thoughts of her came easy then. I realized I had so much of the trail left to hike though, and I got this nervous twitch in my stomach because I thought about her maybe not waiting for me to finish. I had months of hiking still to come, and I drank my coffee as I wrote about the time she and I went to Harper's Ferry in West Virginia to hike and camp for a weekend. We had a blast on that trip, and Harper's Ferry is one of the coolest little places. I started thinking about the possibility of her maybe driving up to meet me somewhere along the trail. That thought was a good way for me to end my writing, so I finished my coffee and headed back to Uncle Johnny's place.

It was getting late in the morning when I got back, and Johnny was all dressed up in his Sunday best. "You clean up well," I said. "Where are you headed?"

"It's Sunday, my good man—church day. Gotta go pay my respects to the Lord and all."

"No kiddin'," I said. "I didn't know Yankee fans went to church."

"Yeah, well, a few of us do, I suppose. I asked the others if they wanted to tag along, and they all said yes, so you're welcome to join us if you like."

"Well, I appreciate the invitation," I said. "Let me think about that for a few."

"Can't think on it for too long," he said, "we're leaving in five minutes."

I went upstairs to the bunk where I had slept, and on top of the bed was my wool hat, all stitched up nicely by Johnny. I picked it up and ran my fingers across the stitching he added, and I appreciated his act of kindness. I'm not sure how or why, but seeing my hat freshly mended like that prompted me to accept his invitation to go to church with him and the others. It's not like I had any nice clothes though, so I splashed some water on my face and put on my least stinky shirt. I met Johnny and the others in the driveway, and we all piled into Johnny's Ford F-150. I sat in the backseat, between Saluki and Coke, and I asked Saluki in a whisper if he normally went to church. "No," he said, "but I'm not sure when I'll get the next chance to go to a Baptist church in Tennessee."

"Good point," I said.

I could hear the music playing and the tambourines clapping when we parked the truck and started walking toward the front of the church. There were small girls in flowered dresses and little boys in button-down shirts with pin-on ties that were running around the church yard screaming and laughing, and Johnny started shaking hands with other church members as we walked behind him. "These are some of my hiker friends," Johnny said to the congregation, and suddenly, all of us hikers were surrounded and welcomed by smiling Baptists. An old southern man in plaid pants and an outdated blazer jacket grabbed my hand with both of his and went on to tell me how excited he was that I was there to attend the service.

"My pleasure," I said, as I struggled a little bit to get my hand back.

Saluki and I chuckled at all the excitement as we followed the flock of believers into the church. Being so dirty and all, we hikers took our seats in the back row of the small church, away from all the others. We knew our clothes and boots didn't smell all that good, so we sat as far away as possible. Johnny sat beside us with a smile on his face.

A hush came over the room as an older gentleman got behind the pulpit and made the special announcement that the James family had come all the way from Johnson City to lead the service that morning. The hundred or so church members all stood up and clapped as the Johnson family made their way to the stage. There was Papa James, Momma James, and their two sons, Luke and Isaiah. Papa James looked proud to introduce his family to everyone, and each member of the family waved and bowed before they took a seat on the side of the stage. I was amazed when Papa James announced that his eighteen-year-old son, Luke, would be giving the sermon that morning, and I think everyone else was amazed too because of the buzz and chatter that came over the crowd with that announcement. I nudged Saluki in the ribs as I tried not to laugh, and everyone watched as Luke adjusted his tie and walked up to the pulpit. "This should be great," I whispered to Saluki.

Luke was tall and thin, and his suit jacket looked a couple sizes too big for him. He had some wet gel in his hair, parted to the left, slicked back, and he hadn't outgrown the acne splotches on his cheeks and chin. His stern look suggested he wanted to be older than he was. "Poor kid," I whispered to Saluki.

The room fell quiet once again as Luke looked around at all the members. There was an extended pause as Luke stood there, and I wondered if he was nervous. He looked very serious for such a young man, and then he put both his hands on the sides of the pulpit as he leaned in over the microphone. "If you do not know Jesus Christ as your own personal savior, then you may never know," he said.

"Mmm-hmm," came from a few members in the crowd.

"If you walk out those doors today," he said, with one hand raised, pointing to the front door, "without turning your life over to Jesus… then you may never get that chance again."

"Amen!" came from several members in the crowd.

"And if you're here today and you haven't turned your life over to Jesus, then I want you to do that right now!"

"You tell'm, preacher!"

Luke's voice started getting louder. "If you're in here today, and you're lost, then the moment has come for you to be found!" Louder still, "If you're in here today, and you're surrounded by darkness, then the moment has come for you to find the light!"

"Hallelujah!" shouted the crowd.

"So," shouted Luke, "if you are ready to accept Jesus Christ into your life, then I want you to come up here with me right now!"

The room fell silent as the heads of the people in front of us started looking around. I could see Luke looking around the room too, and to my surprise, his eyes stopped when he saw the row of poorly dressed hikers in the back.

"I will say it once again," he shouted, looking right at us. "If you are lost, then come on up here and get found!"

"Come on now!" shouted someone in the crowd. "Come on up."

Nobody moved. A couple moments passed. Luke stood firm behind the pulpit. I started getting nervous because I swear Luke was staring right at me. I tried to cover myself by sliding lower in my seat. Luke started up again, "If you have not found Jesus...."

Then someone stood up. It was a young girl in one of the front pews. Luke shifted his stare toward her, and I felt relieved. The crowd began to clap and praise "Amen!" as the girl made her way up front. Papa James and the rest of the family stood and clapped with smiling faces as Luke stood over the kneeling girl in front of him. Everyone in the church stood and praised and clapped and prayed.

"This is something else," I whispered to Saluki.

"You're telling me," he said.

"He was looking right at us!" I said.

"He sure was," said Saluki.

"We need to thank that little girl for saving us," I said.

Saluki laughed at the irony. "Yeah, we do."

The drive back to Uncle Johnny's place was full of chatter because Coke had to tell us about being saved like that some twenty years earlier, and then Shenandoah had to tell us about how close he was to standing up for Luke. "Why didn't ya?" asked Johnny. Shenandoah sidestepped the question by asking Johnny if he had ever been saved like that. Johnny didn't give him a straight answer, but he did say, "I go to that church every Sunday."

Saluki said something about how his family was religious, but not like that, and I didn't say anything about God or Jesus or the church because we hardly went when I was younger.

Johnny let me use his phone before I left his place, and I sat in one of those pine rocking chairs on the front porch when I called Jada. Her voice was soft and sweet when she answered. "I had a feeling you'd call me today," she said. She was in the middle of running her Sunday errands, so she talked to me from inside the Publix grocery store.

"Which isle are you in?" I asked.

"What do you mean?"

"Which isle of the supermarket are you in?" I said.

"The one with the granola bars and oatmeal and maple syrup. Why?"

"It helps me to see you better," I said. "What are you wearing?"

She laughed. "I'm wearing my Burlington, Vermont t-shirt and those pink shorts you like."

"You're right," I said. "You look great in those shorts."

We laughed about that, and then I told her about the church service and how Luke wanted to save us. "I'll save you," she said, in that sexy voice of hers.

"I love how you say that from the granola bar isle!"

"It's lonely pushing this cart all by myself," she said.

"Well, that's part of the reason why I'm calling," I said. I went on to tell her that I'd be in Damascus, Virginia in eight or nine days, and I asked if she had the time to drive up and meet me there. "Do you have any vacation time saved up?" I asked.

"Oh, baby!" she said. "I'd love to come and meet up with you! How exciting! Yeah, I have plenty of time saved up. Hold on," she said, "let me get over here to the bakery section so I can hear you better and work all this out."

I closed my eyes, and I could see her in that section of the store, wearing those clothes. "What's it smell like in the bakery?" I said.

"Like cinnamon rolls and chocolate frosting," she said, laughing.

"Awe, man," I said. "I'd love to have one of those cinnamon rolls!"

"I'll bring you one," she said. "Okay. So, eight or nine days from now would be next Monday or Tuesday and…" She started talking to herself as she worked out the days off and the time it would take her to drive to and from Damascus. She was very excited as she talked everything out to herself, and I just sat there rocking back and forth in Johnny's chair as she went on talking everything out. "Okay," she finally said. "How about I see you at the Creeper Trail Cottages in Damascus next Monday at three o'clock?"

I looked at my trail book and did the math real quick. "That's about fourteen miles of hiking for me each day," I said. "I can do that."

"Oh, baby!" she said. "This is so exciting!"

"The Creeper Trail Cottages?" I said. "Sounds spooky."

She laughed. "Nope. Not spooky at all. There are pictures here that I'm looking at right now on the website, and they're so cute. We can have our own little cottage all to ourselves!" she said.

"That sounds amazing," I said.

"Oh, I love you," she said.

"I love you too, baby."

Andy and I used to hang out a lot at the train tracks near our house. There's a bridge there in the woods with a small river that runs underneath, and we used to play there by the river's edge and throw rocks at empty bottles. Andy got his hands on a bee-bee gun one time, and we collected empty bottles from nearby trash cans so we could have more targets to shoot at. We spent a lot of time down by that river, and I wonder if Andy thought about those times at all when he sat by the Nolichucky River.

13

The hike out of Erwin was bumpy and slow going. The trail zigged and zagged its way along, and loose rocks were everywhere. I had to watch every step because it would have been easy to twist or sprain an ankle. I thought a lot about Uncle Johnny's generosity, and I'll be honest, I couldn't understand why a beer drinking, cigarette smoking Yankee fan would want to go to that church every week. Those Tennessee Baptists were something else!

I'm not sure how long I thought about that; it was a while, because the sun had shifted its way across the sky in the meantime. I just couldn't figure out what Uncle Johnny saw in that church. I mean, I could see how Johnny's face lit up when he was talking to all the hikers at his place and around his table, but I didn't see his face light up like that while we were at his church. Maybe it was because he wasn't in *his* house? Maybe he acted differently in *God's* house? Who knows? Maybe he wasn't a huge fan of all the pride and ego on the faces of the James family, or the harsh condemning warnings from Luke. I also wondered if Johnny wanted me and the other hikers to stand up and kneel before that pimply-faced kid. I wasn't sure about all that, and I started to care less and less about it, because the one thing I did know for sure was that I was on my way to Damascus to see my girl. Man, I was excited to see her! Now that I had something like that to look forward to, the hiking became much easier to handle. All I had to do was hike fourteen miles a day, and eight days later, she'd be there.

I could hear all the chatter before I could see anybody. As I approached Overmountain Shelter, their voices grew louder, and it sounded like an army of teenagers. Then the trail opened up to a large grassy meadow, and in the far corner of the field was a huge barn that had been converted into Overmountain Shelter. There were young people everywhere. I walked over and said hello to a man standing outside the barn, and he had a whistle around his neck and a name tag that said *Jerry*, so I figured he was someone in charge.

Jerry was nice enough, but he had a frantic look on his face as he continuously looked around. I could tell he was trying to keep an eye on all the kids coming and going from the barn, but he didn't look very comfortable or confident. I asked Jerry what was going on, and he said that he was sponsoring an outreach program for high school kids. "We're out here for three days to do some nature hikes and camping," he said, "and we just got here about an hour ago, so we're still a little disorganized."

"Well," I said, "I was planning on spending the night in this shelter, so you think that will be a problem?"

"No, no, no," he said. "Most of the kids have tents that they will pitch outside the barn, and anyone who does sleep inside will be on the first floor. So, if you're okay with sleeping in the loft, then you're more than welcome. Help yourself."

I thanked Jerry and went inside the barn. What a cool place it was! It was huge. Fifty people could have easily slept in that place. There was a wooden staircase in the back corner that took me up to the loft, and I found a great spot right near the open window to set myself up for the night. The floor of the loft was made out of wide wooden planks, so there were small gaps between the boards where I could see through. I could see the heads of the kids below me as they came and went from the barn, and I could hear their conversations about whether they wanted to sleep in the barn or out in a tent. They all seemed very excited to be there, and most of them decided to sleep outside in a tent. I figured it would end up being pretty quiet in the barn after all.

"But she's a douche bag," I heard one girl say to another girl. "And if she doesn't watch herself, I'm gonna beat her ass!"

I leaned forward and looked through the gap in the floor to see the heads of the two girls talking. I laughed to myself, as I started putting together my dinner on my stove.

"But you'll get kicked out of the retreat if you do anything to her," her friend said. "They'll make you go home."

"I don't care," said the girl. "If she was messing around with my boyfriend, then I'm gonna beat her ass."

The two girls walked out of the barn, and I could see them through the open window of the loft as they walked over to another group of girls trying to pitch a tent. I couldn't hear them anymore, but I could tell from their body language and the way they moved their hands that they were still talking about whipping that girl's ass.

For a while, I thought I would be the only hiker in the loft that night. It was nice to sit by the open window, smoke my cigarettes, and write in my journal. But then I heard someone coming up the stairs of the loft, and it was a hiker I hadn't met before. He introduced himself as Garcia, and he said no when I asked if he was a thru-hiker. "I'm just out here for a week or so to get some fresh air and clear my head."

"Where you from?" I asked.

"Tennessee," he said. "Near Shady Valley, a little north of here. I had a buddy drop me off near Iron Mountain Gap yesterday afternoon, and I'm basically hiking back home."

"Sounds like a cool little trip," I said.

"Yeah, I did this same trip a few years ago, and it was great, so I took some time from work, and here I am."

Garcia was a dark-haired, olive-skinned guy around thirty, and he had thick eyebrows and high cheek bones. He had the name *Maria* tattooed on the side of his neck, and he said it was his daughter's name when I asked him about it. He said Maria was four years old, still too young to hike with him, but he looked forward to the time when she could come with him. Garcia's eyes got big and bright when he talked about Maria, but then he started talking about how things with his wife weren't going so well. "We're struggling for money these days," he said, "and my wife wants to move back to Texas, where her family is. But I don't want to go there," he said. "Her family doesn't like me all that much."

He and I talked for a while longer, and I told him about hiking to Damascus to meet up with Jada. He asked if I had any kids, and I said I didn't. I told him about Uncle Johnny's hostel and the Sunday church service in Erwin, and we both laughed when I told him about little man Luke staring at me from behind the pulpit. "Did you get up and get saved?" asked Garcia.

"Hell, no!" I said.

Garcia shook his head and chuckled to himself. "I don't know about people these days," he said.

I told him about the butterflies I saw on the trail and how they let me get close to them. I told him about the little funeral they had for their fallen friend, and I didn't embellish the story like I did with Tucker.

"No shit?" said Garcia.

"No shit," I replied. "True story."

Garcia told me about his daughter's birthday party a few months earlier and how his wife bought her some of those fairy wings that she found online. "Maria could strap them onto her back like she was a fairy herself," he said. "And it was so funny to watch her run around the house with those things on. She was so cute, but then she actually thought she could fly, and she ran out onto the back porch and jumped off the stairs thinking she'd take off and fly like Peter Pan or something."

"Oh shit!" I said. "What happened to her?"

Garcia laughed. "She landed in a snowbank and started crying. It was crazy, man. My wife ended up taking those wings away from her because she wouldn't stop jumping off things. The couch. The bed. It was crazy. But I was reminded of those fairy wings when you started talking about the colored wings of the butterflies you saw on the trail."

"Maria sounds like a great little kid," I said.

"The love of my life," said Garcia. "The love of my life."

I woke up early the next morning to a few kids talking outside the barn. They weren't being all that loud, but their noise was enough to wake me. Garcia was still crashed out while I made my morning coffee, and I thought about maybe hiking along with him for the week, but I decided against it because I had a deadline to meet and I didn't want to get slowed down. I wished Garcia well in a little note that I left on his pack, and I had to walk on my tiptoes to avoid waking up several teenagers asleep on the first floor of the barn.

Jada took up so many of my thoughts that morning as I hiked along, and going over Little Hump Mountain made me think of her even more. Funny how things work that way—I was horny as hell hiking over those mountains!

I found myself stuck between two shelters that day, so I had to make a decision on how far I wanted to hike. I could take a short day and only hike eight miles to Apple House Shelter, where I'd probably see Garcia again, or I could take a long day and hike the twenty-three miles to Moreland Gap Shelter. Those were my two choices. I knew I got an early start, and the terrain wasn't so bad, so I opted for the long day to Moreland Gap. Slow and steady was my plan, and I knew I'd get there by nightfall if I kept a steady pace.

Jada and I only camped together once, and that was the trip we took to Harper's Ferry a month or so before I started hiking the trail. I had done some reading about Harper's

Ferry when I first researched the Appalachian Trail, and I was intrigued by the Civil War history tied to that place— you know, John Brown and all. It was a place I couldn't wait to check out, and Jada said that Harper's Ferry wasn't that far from where her sister was living in Frederick, Maryland. So, after we talked to her sister and after I bought all the hiking gear for my big trip, we drove up to her sister's place for a few days to visit and to do some hiking around Harper's Ferry. And it was great too because it gave me a chance to break in all my new gear, like the collapsible stove I bought, my tent, my new sleeping bag, and especially the new boots I got. I needed to break in those boots and practice using all my other stuff before I left for the trail. I wanted to know what it was like to hike a few miles with a full pack.

It was mid-February when we got to her sister's place, so the weather was still pretty cold for hiking, but after I begged and pleaded with Jada, she finally agreed that we could spend one night camping in the tent at Harper's Ferry. The other nights would be spent at her sister's place. I never thought Jada would go for a night outdoors in February, so I was surprised when she said she'd do it. She wasn't nearly as excited as I was though.

Harper's Ferry is a small town wedged between the Shenandoah and Potomac rivers. Many of the houses and buildings there have been converted into Civil War museums and historical sites, and it has that wartime 1860s feel to it. Lots of graveyards. We parked our car in the local lot and paid the money to leave it there overnight, and we started hiking around. Maryland was to the north, Virginia to the south, and we were standing in West Virginia, so it was cool to be standing in a place where three different states came together like that. Then I saw one of the painted white blazes marked on a tree, about eight inches long, and I got this anxious feeling in my gut because that blaze marked the Appalachian Trail. It was exciting to know that I'd soon be hiking that trail for real, following those white blazes like breadcrumbs for twenty-two hundred miles.

After hiking near the rivers for a while, Jada wanted to do some window shopping in the center of town, and it was a pain in the ass to take that pack off every time she wanted to go into a store. There weren't many stores open that time of year, but those that were, she wanted to go in. So, taking that pack off and putting it back on every time we went inside a place was pretty annoying, but I never said anything to her because she'd just laugh and say something sarcastic about me needing to carry that thing around with me every day for the next six months. And she'd be right too, so I just didn't say anything.

It was cold that day, and the wind was blowing at a pretty good clip, so after we shopped in every place she could find, we started hiking north into Maryland. But, of course, it wasn't long before she needed to use the bathroom, and when I told her to pee in the woods, she said she didn't have to pee. So, we turned around and hiked back to the center of town so she could use the restroom at the coffee shop.

The clouds started rolling in, and we could smell the snow in the air, so we needed to find a place to camp for the night. My trail book said the nearest shelter was five miles to the north, and I knew she wouldn't be up for that long of a hike, so we needed to find a place nearby where we could pitch our tent. We decided to head south because it looked less congested, and I thought we might be able to find a field or a patch of woods somewhere secluded.

It started snowing. Then it started snowing harder. We couldn't find a place to camp anywhere. We hiked about a mile south, but there wasn't a place to pitch the tent. She started sighing loudly enough for me to hear, so we turned around and started hiking back toward town. "Maybe we should just drive back to my sister's," she said.

I didn't say anything in response. We kept hiking. The snow was getting heavy. Then I stopped at the top of a hill just south of Harper's Ferry and read the historical marker for the ruins of an old church, the St. John's Episcopal church. She stopped and read the marker with me. I took off my pack and climbed over the little fence. She told me not to, but I did it anyway. I went inside the church, and I could see where the altar once was. The floors of the church were long gone, just like the roof, and I was standing on flat ground. It made absolute sense to me… "We can camp right here," I said.

"No way," she said. "You're not supposed to be in there," she said. "That's a historical church site, not a campsite."

"But it's flat ground," I said. "And it's getting late. Listen, we're both hungry, and it's friggin' cold, so let's just pitch the tent here, eat dinner, and then we can get warm inside the tent. Nobody is gonna see us and nobody is gonna care," I said.

She started looking around to see if anyone was watching us. There wasn't anybody around. She knew the sun was close to setting. She knew it was cold and getting colder. She knew she was hungry. I just stood inside the church and watched her as she took a few minutes to think things through. "Fine," she eventually said. "But we're gonna get kicked out of here, and it's all gonna be all your fault!" She handed me my pack, and then she climbed over the little fence. "I don't know why we just don't go back to my sister's," she said.

The tent was super easy to set up and my new stove worked great. It wasn't long before we were getting warm on chicken soup and Italian bread. We couldn't believe how much snow had fallen that afternoon—three or four inches anyway—but it was starting to taper off as we cleaned the pots and dishes after dinner. From our view on top of the hill, it looked like all of Harper's Ferry was covered in a clean white blanket of snow.

It felt great to snuggle up together inside the tent, but it took a while to get situated and warm. Two people in a one-person tent is tricky to maneuver, but we managed. We were both wearing all the clothes we brought, and the one sleeping bag we had was tough to share, but it all worked out. We kept each other warm. It was soothing to listen to the tree limbs sway and creak outside the tent, and once the clouds began to clear, the moon came out, and we could see those same tree limbs dancing through the fabric of the tent. "I can't believe we're camping in the ruins of an old Civil War church," she said.

"Would you like to pray?" I said, laughing.

It was around one in the morning when we heard footsteps in the snow. They woke both of us up, and we could hear the steps getting closer and closer to the tent. Her face was right next to mine, and I could see her eyes growing bigger and more nervous. I reached for my pocketknife and held it in my hand. The footsteps got closer, each step packing down the snow, and then they stopped, right at the base of the tent. We waited for someone to speak. We waited to hear the voice of some park ranger telling us that we were trespassing and had to leave. We waited longer. And longer. Nobody spoke. We could feel the presence of someone standing right outside the tent, and our fear quickly turned to fright. Those were agonizing moments, terrifying actually, and after a minute or so of silence, she whispered, "Aren't you gonna go check it out?"

I had zero interest in checking anything out, but I knew it needed to be done. I knew someone was right outside the tent though, so I put on my headlamp and gripped my knife. I slowly unzipped the tent. My heart was pounding through my chest, and her hands were shaking as she clutched my arm. Slowly, I peeled open the tent. I was ready to pounce, but I feared being pounced upon. My headlamp light bounced off the snow, and I couldn't see anyone standing there. I decided to jump out of the tent as quickly as I could. She let go of my arm, and I leapt out, knife in hand.

The moonlight was almost as bright as my headlamp. The blanket of white snow on the ground allowed me to see everything around me. There wasn't anyone there. I looked around the perimeter of the church and there wasn't anybody there either. I looked down at the snow, shining my light, and I couldn't see any footprints. I was baffled, but relieved. I was standing in the exact spot where the footsteps were, but there was nothing. No tracks in the snow. Crazy. I walked outside the church and around the church, no tracks. I walked over to the trailhead, no tracks.

I went back to the tent and turned my headlamp off. I stood there… I don't know how long… waiting for something. But nothing came.

I unzipped the tent and crawled back inside. Jada was coiled up in a ball at the back of the tent. "It's okay," I told her. "We're fine. It's okay," I said.

"Who's there?" she said in a whisper.

I paused. I didn't know how to tell her that nothing was there because I heard it just like she did. "Nobody," I said. "There isn't anybody there."

She lunged forward in the tent, finger pointed right in my face. "You know just as well as I do that somebody was there. They were standing right fucking there!"

"I know, I know," I said. "But I just walked around this entire church, and there isn't one footprint other than mine in the snow."

"What the fuck!" she said. "That's impossible."

"I know. I can't believe it either. But nobody's there," I said again.

We ended up packing everything up at two in the morning because there was no way either of us could sleep after that. We were thoroughly spooked, as we should have been, and the car ride back to her sister's place in Frederick was quiet. Neither of us knew what to say. There was nothing really to say.

Jada woke me up the next morning around ten by shaking my arm. "Baby," she said. "Baby, wake up."

"What?" I said. "Everything okay?"

"Come on, baby, wake up," she said. "You gotta see this."

"See what?" I said, sitting up.

"This," she said. "You gotta read this. I woke up this morning and I *had* to look into that church, so I started searching around online and look at what I found." She handed me her sister's laptop.

"Can I have some coffee first?" I said.

"No!" she said, slapping my arm. "Read."

I cleared my eyes and started to read. She had found a few articles and passages from books that talked about the church on top of the hill just south of Harper's Ferry. There was a picture of the church ruins where we tried to sleep, and then there were different accounts and testimonies from people who claimed to have encountered the ghost of Father Costello—the priest who once ran that congregation before the church burned to the ground in the 1860s. "It was the ghost of Father Costello!" she said. "You know, just like I do, that something was there last night, and that's who it was! It was the ghost of Father Costello!" she said.

1:27am

I found the blue jay in the attic about an hour ago. He was hiding in the back corner, wedged behind an old desk and a few boxes of old clothes. He started to shiver when I went to pick him up, but he let me do it anyway. I climbed back down the rickety ladder stairs and walked over to the front door of the house. It was quiet in the house; mother was already asleep, and I could hear the ticking of the old grandfather clock in the living room. The bird remained quiet in my hands. I took him out onto the front porch, and he didn't try to escape my grip when he knew he was outside. I opened my hands and watched as he gathered himself and flew away.

It's hard to read through these stories that I wish my brother told me in person. I went back to the attic to finish reading.

14

It was hard to sleep because I was only ten miles away from seeing her. I kept tossing and turning in my sleeping bag, and the hardwood floor of the shelter felt harder than usual. I sat up often and smoked. I thought about Garcia several times throughout the day, especially when I hiked past Shady Valley, and I wondered if his time in the woods gave him what he was looking for. I smoked on that thought for a while. Abingdon Gap Shelter was quiet that night, and I was sleeping alone again. It was loud between my ears but quiet in the forest. The moon was hidden behind tree branches, now filled with new leaves, but it would find ways to peek through and cast light on the shelter floor. I watched the smoke from my cigarette spiral upward as I exhaled my cloud into the night. I could hear Jada's voice talking to me, and I could see that gorgeous smile of hers— she was only ten miles away.

It was a little after two in the afternoon when I got there. I made good time with my hike that morning. The front office clerk at the Creeper Trail Cottages told me that a young lady had already checked in to cottage number five, and when I started walking that way, I could see her leaning against the front porch post of our cottage with arms folded across her chest. She looked very sexy in that pose. My walk over to her was slow and deliberate. Her smile was big and beautiful. When I was about twenty feet from her, she unfolded her arms and came running over to me. I dropped my pack where I stood and wrapped both my arms around her. "Oh, my God," she said. "It's so good to see you."

I didn't say anything. I just hugged her. She started kissing my neck and my cheeks. She ran her fingers through my hair and then my beard. She kissed me again. Then, with both hands on my cheeks, she looked me in the eyes, breathed deep, and told me that I smelled awful. We both laughed. "I need a shower pretty bad," I said.

"I'd like to take one with you," she said. "I'll even wash your back for you."

Our cottage was cute and cozy, and we filled it with laughter and naked time and good takeout food from the local Chinese place. It was easier than I thought it would be to talk to her about the trail and the good time I was having. She wanted to hear about all of it, and we laughed and I smoked and we laughed some more, especially when I reenacted my drive with belt buckle Bob and tried to speak in his voice. Jada said she wanted to meet Jeff and Nancy because they sounded like genuine, good-hearted people. I told her we could plan a drive up to spend the weekend with them if she wanted, and she liked that idea. I tried to sing Violet's song for her, but she was too busy laughing at me singing naked in front of her on the bed. I stuck my gut way out in front of me, as far as I could, as I tried to act like Old Smoky on the balcony, thanking her for the song.

"You're too funny," she said. "The one question I do have for you though, is whether or not you've met any other ghosts like Father Costello?"

"Nope," I said. "No ghosts. Just a lot of really cool people that I can't imitate very well."

Neither of us wanted to hike or walk around too much, so the next morning we drove around Damascus and drank coffee as I waited for my clothes to dry at the local laundromat. I was pleasantly surprised when she brought some of my sweatpants and sweatshirts with her, and the soft cotton on my skin felt dreamy. She even brought me fresh underwear and socks. I kissed her face up and down and thanked her. "You're the best," I said.

I woke up in the middle of the night because I heard her coughing in the bathroom. I asked if she was alright, and through the closed bathroom door she said she was okay. "Just not feeling so good," she said. A few minutes later she crawled back into bed and said that something she ate must not have agreed with her.

She felt better the next morning though, so we ate homemade hash and scrambled eggs at the Damascus Diner. We got extra bacon and sourdough toast, and we both cleaned our plates. "I'm so stuffed," she said, rubbing her belly.

We drove by The Broken Fiddle Hostel to see if any thru-hikers were staying there, but we were too late to meet Saluki and Shenandoah because they had already left. She thought it was sweet when I told her about the crush Shenandoah had on Violet. "Yeah," I said, "but he's like fifty, and she's like nineteen."

"Oh," she said, somewhat shocked. "That's gross."

We walked around Damascus Town Park after that, but that's when our laughter started to fade because we both knew the time for her to leave was upon us. "Goodbyes have never really been my thing," she said, "so be safe and know that I love you. And please call me sometime this week."

I stood on the front porch of cottage number five, and I watched as she got into her car and wiped the tears away from her eyes. She blew me a kiss through the windshield, and I blew one back. "Thank you for the wonderful time," she said, through her cracked window as she pulled away.

I only had a half hour before checkout time, so I went back inside the cottage and started to pull my things together. I rolled up all my freshly washed clothes and stored them away in my pack. I organized my food bag. I picked up the dirty towels on the floor of the bathroom and made sure the cottage was somewhat clean. Then I reached for my boots… and that's when I saw the note she left me. She left it in my boot because, of course, I'd find it there, and I sat on the corner of the bed as I unfolded the paper and read her words.

She again thanked me for such a wonderful time in cottage number five, but then she said there was something she needed to tell me. "I didn't want to tell you this while I was with you," she wrote, "because I didn't want our visit to be all about it. I love you very much," she said, "and I know you still have months of hiking ahead of you, but I need to tell you that I'm pregnant. I found out a couple weeks ago, and I know the timing isn't great, but we're going to have a baby," she wrote, "and I love the idea of us being parents together…."

The note started to twitch in my hands, and the sudden lump in my throat made it hard to swallow and breathe. I can't recall a time in my life where I cried and laughed at the same time, but during that moment, the fear and the joy all came together at once. Instinctively, I wanted to be angry, but I wasn't angry. I wished she had told me about it in person, but I wasn't upset she didn't. The fear I started to feel was heavy and thick, and I could feel it trying to encase my heart. I didn't want that, but I did feel it. So many thoughts flashed so quickly, like they were being poured over me—my deadbeat father, the need for money with a child, the commitment, the pressure, the forever—I had to stand up and force myself to breathe deep—slow and easy.

The joy I felt came more in the form of *another opportunity*, and the thoughts of Sue Cummings and our son flooded over me, making me view this new pregnancy with Jada as a second chance to be present and engaged and responsible. I could still taste the hatred I had toward my own father for not being present and responsible with us, and I didn't want it to be like that with me. I needed to talk myself away from those feelings of anger and those thoughts of hatred. *I don't have to be like my father.*

The fear inside tried to steal the joy because I could sense it and I could feel it, so I consciously forced those two different emotions to separate corners of my soul. I didn't want that fear-filled-joy to be at war within my gut because I knew it would affect what I saw and how I saw it. It would influence everything, and I didn't want to make any of my decisions through those lenses. On one hand, I wanted to shout out from the rooftops with joy, but on the other hand, I wanted to curl up someplace and cry. I wanted to thank someone for this second chance, but I also wanted to run away and be alone in the woods. I wanted to walk out that cabin door right then and hike all those feelings away, but I also wanted to pull up a chair, drink coffee, and write out everything I felt. I felt like I could have hiked one hundred miles that day, but I also felt like I could've written a book about all of it… *I could write a book about all if it.*

The front desk clerk said that cottage number five was still available if I wanted it. I asked how long I could rent it for, and he told me that two weeks was the maximum allowed. I told him I wanted it for a week, but probably for two. "No problem," he said. "If you want to extend your stay for another week, just let us know before the first week is over."

I went over to the local supermarket and bought a few supplies. I bought extra coffee, sugar, cream, deli meats, cheese, mayo, and bread. They had a stationary section in one of the isles, so I bought a couple of new pens, black ink, and a three pack of yellow legal pads. I also bought a carton of Marlboro Reds and a new lighter.

It was the thought that I could write a book about everything that stuck with me. Out of all the feelings and emotions and thoughts I had swirling around inside, it was the thought that I *should* write it all down that won out. It just made sense to me. I went back to cottage number five, and I pulled my journal from my backpack. I read it from start to finish, and I recapped everything that the Appalachian Trail had given me up to that point. I fixed myself a sandwich and I sat on the front porch as I ate. I smoked a cigarette after that, and I could feel the food digesting in my stomach as the thoughts marinated in my mind. The story I would write started to take shape. I finished my cigarette and I went back inside.

I started with the day I left Jada in Jacksonville because that seemed like the right place to begin. It was easy to write about loving her and leaving her to hike in the woods, but it was hard to write about Robert driving me up to the trailhead. I mean, he wasn't dead back then, but he was dead when I wrote those words, so I had to pretend like he was still right there beside me, like I was still talking to him and smoking with him as he drove that piece of shit Honda north through Atlanta. It was hard to write those words.

I had to stop writing after I got the first chapter down on paper because my thoughts were beginning to crowd my mind and jump around from place to place. I went back outside to smoke. The fear and the joy in my belly continued to take turns as they worked on my thinking. The idea of being a father again, for the first time really, overshadowed all my other thoughts, but right behind those thoughts were the thoughts of my own father, which tasted sour and spoiled and rotten. How could I rejoice in being a father myself when I hated my own father at the same time? I smoked.

But then I remembered meeting Rock and Little Rock, and a smile came to my face. A sense of ease came to my chest as I thought about Little Rock stirring his food just like his father did. My fear began to settle down. The weight sitting on my chest began to lift. My thoughts became a little clearer. My breathing became easier. I knew I could write about my father.

I thought of my brother and sister and my mother as well. And suddenly, all sorts of different moments from my past started racing through my mind—partying with my brother, making fun of my sister, arguing with my mother— my mind went from this to that, back and forth, and I felt the insanity of trying to corral all those memories into one organized place. I became overwhelmed and exhausted. I smoked again.

I knew I would leave the trail and go back to Jada in Florida. She needed me there with her, and I wasn't going to miss out on my second opportunity to be a father. I needed to be there through all of it. I would come back to the trail at some point in my life because I needed to finish what I started there as well. I needed to see and feel and experience what the rest of this trail had to offer me.

I went back inside and I grabbed a legal pad that hadn't been written on yet. At the top of the first page, I wrote *Chapter Two*. Then I tore that page away from the pad and placed it on the bed. At the top of the next page, I wrote *Chapter Three*. I tore off that page too and put it on the bed. I did the same thing for chapters four, five, six, and seven. I stopped there. I looked at the bed and stared at the blank 'chapters' of paper. I tossed my journal from the trail onto the bed as well, and then I stood before the bed for a long time, thinking and plotting. I envisioned those chaptered pages full of different bullet points—each bullet point marking an event or a time or something relevant. I began to think about how each piece of paper, each chapter, might overlap and interconnect with the others.

I stepped outside and smoked. I knew I needed a master outline of each chapter—a simple one though.

I went back inside and picked up one page at a time. I knew I would use my time on the Appalachian Trail as the backbone of the story, but I needed to fill in the bullet points of everything else I wanted to say in each chapter. It all needed to fit somehow. So, I started. I filled in some here. I filled in more there. The whole thing started to take shape. I smoked when I had thoughts that needed to be worked out. I kept at it.

The sun was starting to come up because I could see it in the window curtains that started to change color. It took me that whole night and nearly a full pack of cigarettes to finish creating the master outline, and when it was done, there were thirteen different pages on the bed, each page being a different chapter. I no longer felt overwhelmed with the whole story cluttering my mind because I was looking at the whole story laid out on the bed in front of me. I picked up each piece of paper in the correct order and placed the stack on the nightstand beside the bed. I laid down and fell fast asleep.

I woke up thinking about my mother. I hadn't spoken to her in quite some time. I hadn't spoken to anyone in my family for some time, but I woke up thinking about my mother. She had always told me that I was just like my father, and I hated her for that. When I was a kid, she would say I laughed like my father. When I ate, she said I ate like him. And when I drank, she screamed that I drank like him. I never felt like she was looking at me though—just an image of the man she once loved. I couldn't take it anymore. I had to leave home. I said nasty things to her on my way out of town, and that was the last time I spoke to her. But I woke up that morning thinking about her and all of that, so I drank a lot of coffee as I tried to wash those thoughts away.

Chapter Two was easy to write because everything was still fresh in my mind. I could still see the park ranger at Amicalola Falls, and I could still feel my burning lungs on that first day of hiking. That part came easy. It was hard to write about Robert as a living, breathing, friend of mine, so I had to keep playing tricks on my thinking—I couldn't let the sadness of his death distort the brotherhood I felt while he was alive. I couldn't allow those feelings of loss to filter their way into the narrative I was writing, so I pushed those thoughts aside and embraced the laughter and common ground we shared as living friends. I smoked a lot.

Once *Chapter Two* and *Chapter Three* were written, I loved the feeling of crumpling up each of those outlined pages and throwing them in the trashcan. I enjoyed holding the first three chapters in my hands. They had weight to them, and I wanted more of that feeling. The writing came fast in some parts but slow in other parts. I would smoke outside and wonder why certain parts were harder than others to write. I kept thinking about my mother though, and I would push those thoughts of her further down because I wasn't writing about her in that part of the book. But she was there, ever present, as I pushed her away again and pushed on with the writing.

I decided it was time to see her again—my mother that is. It was somewhere around *Chapter Six* when the thoughts of my mother simply became too much. I had difficulty focusing on the writing, so I made that decision. I looked into a bus ticket to Boston, and I bought it the next day. My plan was simple—to finish my writing in cottage number five, and then I would take a bus to Boston and visit her. I would sit with her and talk with her. I would make amends to her, because there was so much wrong with how I treated her. I would try to let those older resentments go, and I would tell her about the good news I had waiting for me in Florida. I would tell her about Jada and my clean time. I would tell her about my job. I would try to put those old hardships to rest, once and for all.

I smoked and I wrote. I ate and I smoked and I wrote. I slept. I dreamed of what I would write next. I drank coffee and I wrote more. I had eight chapters written when I added a second week to my time in cottage number five. They thanked me for the payment. I went and bought another pack of legal pads. I bought turkey and cheese and cookies. I bought another carton of cigarettes. I laughed at times and cried at other times. I was happy to be alone in cottage number five. I paced the floors when I was blocked, but I never smoked inside the cottage. I wanted to, but I didn't. I spent my smoking time on the front porch, planning and crafting what would come next.

I called Jada in Florida and told her about my plans to leave the trail. At first, she told me not to be silly, and that I should finish hiking the trail. I told her my reasons for leaving, and she started to cry. "Give me a couple weeks," I told her. "Let me handle things in Boston, and then I'll be home and we can start our new little family."

"I'm sorry I didn't tell you about the baby when I was there," she said.

"It's okay," I told her. "I understand."

She asked if I was ready to see my mother again, and I told her about how I couldn't stop thinking about her. "Then it's the right time to do it," she said.

"Do you like living in Florida?" I said.

“Why do you ask me that?”

“I don’t know,” I said. “Just thinking about family and the fact that neither of us have any of that in Florida.”

“We can talk more about that when you get home,” she said.

I know I will miss the trail. I’m afraid that I’ll get too busy with life and work and family to come back to it. The *fellowship of the wilderness* became clearer as I wrote about it, and I want more of it. I need more of it. I need to finish what I started on this trail….

15

March 2, 2023

5:43pm

Journal Entry #1:

I was away at school in Pennsylvania when Andy went home to visit my mother in Boston, so I wasn't there to see him. My mother did call me at school though to ask if I could make it home to see him, but I was in the middle of writing a few midterm essays, so I told her I was too busy and couldn't make it.

But that was pretty much a lie. I could've jumped in the car and made it home. I could've done that. But I didn't. And to be honest, I was still really pissed at Andy for bailing on the family like he did and for not keeping in touch with me after he moved down to Florida. So why should I be the one to go out of my way for him? I mean, if Andy called me on the phone himself and said he really wanted to see me, then I probably would've gone home to see him. I would've. But he didn't do that. *Fuck him,* I thought. It was easy for me to decide against going home, and I lied to my mother about why I couldn't make it.

And my mother called me up again after Andy visited with her, and she was all excited to tell me this and that about their visit. She told me about Jada and the pregnancy, about Andy's sobriety, and about his hiking trip along the Appalachian Trail. "He looked like a real Paul Bunyan when he showed up here at the house," she said. "He had a beard and everything."

Then she told me that Andy wanted to move back to Boston and that he wanted to raise his kid around family. "I couldn't believe it when he said that," said my mother. "It was like I was talking to a totally different person," she said. "He was kind and considerate and thoughtful," she said. "It looks like he's doing really good, Jay. It really does."

I couldn't believe it when she told me that. I mean, I don't remember Andy as being thoughtful or kind, let alone sober. He was a fucking drunk, just like our father was. I never thought sobriety would happen to him, and I found it even harder to believe that he wanted to move back to the place he said he'd never come back to.

But I was intrigued. I really was. My mother made it sound like Andy was a changed man, and I gotta say I was curious about that. I figured maybe, just maybe, there was a chance that all the bullshit from the past could be squared up, and we could all be family again. *Like the old days,* I thought.

And God bless my mother! She was so excited about the news of Andy wanting to come home with Jada and the baby. Andy told my mother that he wanted to wait until the kid was born though, before he moved back, so that gave my mother plenty of time to go out and buy a new bed for Andy and Jada and a new crib for the baby. She basically transformed Andy's old bedroom into a mini apartment during that time. My sister even helped her on the weekends. There were new curtains and rugs and sheets on the bed, new lamps and pictures on the wall. She even painted the whole room over, "in a neutral color," laughed my mother.

I was in the middle of wrapping up the first semester of my sophomore year when I got the call from my mother to say that Jada had the baby. It was a little boy, and they decided to name him Maxwell, after Jada's father. He was born on the first day of December 2019, and my mother even made the trip to Florida that Christmas with my sister to meet Jada and the little guy. I didn't take that trip with my mother and sister to meet Jada and Maxwell though, because money was tight on my end, and I had a bunch of shit to deal with at school.

But honestly, that's another lie, because I could've found the time to do that too. I could've gone down to Florida with them, but I didn't. And I'm not sure what was going on between Andy and me during that time, but it was like some big pissing contest between brothers. It was like, who was gonna be the one to make the first move, me or him? Who was gonna be the brother to break down and reach out to the other? I knew I wasn't gonna be the one to do it, because *fuck him* I thought. I mean, he wronged me way worse than I ever did him, so if he wanted to see me or talk to me, then he could pick up the phone and reach out to me. It sure as hell wasn't gonna be me to do it though.

And my mother and sister were both so friggin' happy when they came back from that Florida trip. Both called me up on the phone and texted me pictures of Maxwell, Jada and Andy. "Isn't he so cute," said my sister, about one of the pictures she sent of Maxwell sleeping. And, "I wish you could've made the trip with us," said my mother. "It really was a lot of fun."

Andy did look different though, and happy, in the pictures I saw of him. I mean, Jada was beautiful, and Maxwell was wicked cute, with his chubby little cheeks and full head of curly hair, but it really burned me up when my sister sent along a picture of all of them together in a big *family* photo with the Christmas tree behind them and all. I mean, I knew that I was still pissed at my brother for not reaching out to me, and for not personally inviting me to Florida with the others, but I also knew that I would never say anything about that to my mother or my sister. I figured that Andy and me had plenty of time to work through all that bullshit from the past when he moved back home, so I just kept all that shit to myself. And honestly, I felt fine about lying to my mother and sister about why I couldn't make the trip down south with them.

The plan was for those guys to move back to Boston in February or March of 2020. Andy talked to my mother about renting a big U-Haul and driving it up, with Jada following behind him in her car with Maxwell. My mother reminded Andy that she already outfitted his old room for them and that they should just sell what they could down in Florida to make the trip up north as simple as possible. They went back and forth about that for a while, but Andy ultimately decided to bring all their stuff with them anyway. And I could tell that that rubbed my mother the wrong way. I could tell she felt a little unappreciated for all the work she did to that bedroom, and for all the shit she bought them. She called me up on the phone one Sunday night telling me about how she couldn't understand why they just couldn't get rid of their stuff down in Florida to make the trip to Boston that much easier. "I mean, I remodeled the whole room for them," she said. "They really don't really need to bring anything at all, except for their clothes and such. But that brother of yours," said my mother, "he's still as stubborn as ever, and your sister came over this weekend to help me move all that stuff I bought up to the attic."

"Jesus!" I said. "Why didn't you wait for me to come home over the break to move all that stuff?"

"Oh, I don't know," she said. "Your sister was here, and we managed alright, I suppose."

"It must've been a bitch getting all that stuff up to the attic."

My mother laughed. "Yeah, your sister and I banged into a few walls and dropped a few things, but like I said, we managed alright."

"Well, maybe Andy and Jada will take that stuff you bought with them when they get a place of their own."

"Yeah, maybe," she said. "But if you need a new futon or a nightstand in the meantime, you're more than welcome to take any of that stuff up to school with you."

I thanked her for the offer, but I had no interest in lugging a bunch of furniture back to school with me.

March 3, 2023

8:23am

Journal Entry #2:

News of Covid spread pretty quick, and I was pissed when my school decided to go remote and I couldn't go back to my dorm. I stayed with my mother in the meantime, and it was tough taking my classes online. Everyone acted like the end of the world was coming, and the lockdowns drove everyone a little nuts. Some people on TV were complaining about their rights being taken away, while other people were talking about how important it was not to see anybody or touch anybody. "Wear a mask!" they said. It was a real shit show, and I watched the news every night with my mother. CNN would say one thing, FOX News would say something else.

Andy called my mother to postpone the move back home, and that was a good thing too, because it would have been tough trying to study with him and Jada and the baby around. But then the hospitals started to fill up with Covid patients, and people started dying from this thing. Every night on the news, they would post the numbers of people who died, and it was crazy how fast those numbers grew.

Jada was the first to get Covid, but then Andy got it a few days after she did. Jada was sick in bed for a couple weeks, but then she came around and started feeling better. My mother was horrified and scared about the baby and all of them being sick, and I was getting pretty scared about it too. My mother and I would watch the news, and she would cry when the stories came on about people who couldn't be with their loved ones as they died in hospital beds.

And this is where I gotta stop because I don't know how to talk about the rest of it…

March 3, 2023
3:47pm

Journal Entry #3:

Fuck it! Andy stayed sick for a long time, and he ended up in the hospital. He was really sick, respiratory sick, and my mother would talk to Jada on the phone every day about how he was doing. Jada said that Andy had moments of consciousness where he would talk to her, saying how much he loved her and all. He said he wanted to talk to me though… and that's the part that's really fucking hard… *he said he wanted to talk to me.*

I withdrew from school after Andy died. I just couldn't fucking handle it. It was tough being alone in the house with my mother. And yeah, my sister would come by for visits sometimes, but it was still tough. I went on walks around the neighborhood alone, and my mother did the same. It took a long time to sort out everything with Andy's death in Florida, and my mother would cry in her bed every night because she couldn't be there in person. She felt so helpless. I cried too, but I did that alone and never in front of my mother.

Jada and Maxwell eventually came to Boston so we could have a proper funeral for Andy. It was a nice service and all, but it was rough meeting the little guy like that. He looks so much like Andy… I still don't like talking about it.

I don't know, I'm not big into coincidences, but I like to think that someone put that blue jay up in the attic after Andy's funeral that day. I mean, if that never happened, then I never would have gone up there, and I never would have seen Andy's backpack sitting there next to the bed my mother bought him and Jada. And as I went through his pack, emptying everything out onto the attic floor, there was this stack of legal pads held together by a few rubber bands. There were five legal pads in all, all numbered and in order, and that's when I started reading. I couldn't believe Andy wrote a book.

It was around Christmas time when I decided to take this trip, and my mother thought it was a great idea when I told her about it. So, like Andy, I went to the local high school and climbed the fucking bleacher stairs at the football field for a few weeks in the cold to try and get myself in shape. And I went to the REI store and bought myself a few things, but I decided to use Andy's pack rather than buying one of my own. I'm happy I did that.

My mother brought Maxwell with her to drop me off at the bus station, and I thought that was cool. He's a very cool little man. Then I got on the bus, and it took me to Damascus, Virginia. I arrived yesterday afternoon, and when I checked into the Creeper Trail Cottages, they said that room number five was already taken, so I got room number six instead. It's a nice little cottage, and I like the front porch, but I'd be a liar if I said I wasn't a little uncomfortable being here. I'm gonna take Andy's advice though, and I'm gonna write about things as they happen to me. My sister gave me a nice leather-bound journal and a couple Pilot G2 pens, and I thanked her very much for that.

When I wake up tomorrow morning, I will strap on that pack of my brother's, and I will pick up where he left off on the Appalachian Trail. I feel good about tomorrow, and I feel good about what I'm doing. I figure it's the least I could do for my brother, Andy. And who knows, maybe our paths will cross somewhere along the way. My trail name is Bluejay, and I look forward to finishing what my brother started.